D1100880

THE COYOTE KIDS

When Billy Bartram met Della Rhodes, he was led to contact her brother, Sandy East, one of the Coyote Kids. Billy's determined vendetta against Long John Carrick — a veteran renegade and gang leader — made him an ally of the Coyote Kids. Carrick's boys were hounding them to grab some valued treasure, but only the Kids knew of its location. When Red Murdo, the other Kid became a casualty, Sandy and Billy had to fight for their very existence ... as well as for the treasure.

DAVID BINGLEY

THE
COYOTE
KIDS

Complete and Unabridged

LINFORD
Leicester

First published in Great Britain in 1970

First Linford Edition
published 2007

British Library CIP Data

Bingley, David, *1920–*
    The Coyote Kids.—Large print ed.—
Linford western library
    1. Western stories
    2. Large type books
    I. Title II. Adams, Bart, *1920–*
823.9′14 [F]

    ISBN 978–1–84617–697–5

Published by
F. A. Thorpe (Publishing)
Anstey, Leicestershire

Set by Words & Graphics Ltd.
Anstey, Leicestershire
Printed and bound in Great Britain by
T. J. International Ltd., Padstow, Cornwall

1

The three-pole corral of the Box W horse ranch in Lordsburg County, south-western New Mexico territory, was clouded with swirling dust. No less than eight cowboys, the owner, Norm Wales, and his two sons were lining the outside of the corral watching the all-out efforts of an agile young man on a half-wild red-eyed pinto.

The beast had been captured some ten days earlier, and this far none of the Box W hands had succeeded in mastering it.

On its back at this time, and risking life and limb against the advice of the rancher, was a young man in his middle twenties. Billy Bartram, the rider in question, was a slim compact individual with thick, short, fair hair and tapering sideburns.

As the pinto bucked and plunged

under him, Billy hung on with his jaw clenched and his chest heaving. His fat-crowned black stetson had acquired a sheen of dust. It remained on his head due to perspiration and a thin leather thong which was tight under his chin.

His grey shirt no longer looked new under the covering of dust, and even the red bandanna at his throat had lost its brightness.

'Attaboy, Billy!' one of the hands yelled. 'Why don't you ride him facin' the tail an' see how he likes that?'

This was scarcely a serious suggestion. Every few seconds the watchers gasped in wonder at the way the resolute young man stayed in the saddle. Time and again he had almost been unshipped, and his performance in retaining his seat almost matched that of the best riders in the Box W bunch.

The pinto snorted, changed direction and hurled itself against the fence directly in front of Rancher Wales and his oldest son, Harvey. Both men stepped back and held their breath in case the rider was thrown against the substantial poles.

At that last minute the pinto checked itself, dug in its shoes and made a turn which merely brushed Billy's leg against the woodwork. Back into the middle they careered, with the cayuse working its fore and hind legs as though they were on some huge series of cords, like a marionette.

Billy looked the worse for wear. His hat had slipped forward and his shoulders were taking the brunt of the jerking. His abdomen hit the saddle horn, but he did not feel the sharp jab of pain immediately. He was preparing for the next trick. The pinto went into a turn, leapt high on all four legs and did the same thing in reverse.

Norm Wales gripped the arm of his son, Harvey.

'Son, I sure as hell am glad the Reverend ain't here to see his boy's performance on that bronco! I don't rightly think he'd ever forgive me for what I've done to Billy, in lettin' him get up there!'

Big-boned Harvey chuckled. 'You're worrying too much, Pa. The Reverend never brought up his boy to be a softy. Besides, Billy insisted on havin' his try. It would have been downright unfriendly not to let him have a go!'

The rancher took his eyes off the arena for a few seconds. He glanced down the private approach track, and saw a distant buckboard approaching.

'Well, glory be, here comes the Reverend, right now. We'll hear about this in a few minutes, an' that's for sure!'

Harvey turned and confirmed his father's findings, but he took a less serious view of the happening. 'It's too late to stop the bustin' now, Pa! The Reverend will jest have to see what's goin' on. After all, there ain't nothin' in the good book against this sort of sport. Is there?'

Having made his statement, Harvey sounded doubtful, but his father was in no mood to answer. He was more than ever intent upon seeing the outcome of the struggle in the corral. As the action came to a climax, he ground his teeth, working the jaw muscles in his mahogany-coloured face, and furtively massaging his big ears.

The pinto had tried to roll Billy before him. On this second attempt to pin him to the earth, the rider was a little more spent. He managed to get his leg out of the stirrup before the animal actually rolled, but immediately after that he failed to find the stirrup again. Consequently, at the next leap, he was half unseated. That brought about the beginning of his downfall.

Shaking its rump as though its backbone was made of india rubber, the pinto triumphantly hurled him out of leather and sent him ploughing up the dust in the direction of the poles. Snickering wickedly, the horse came after him. He rose to his knees, made as if to race for the fence, and at the last minute pulled back.

The beast missed him and before it could return he had gained the nearest part of the fence, and climbed beyond its reach. On the topmost pole he slowed up and held on while his lungs worked like bellows to get his body back to normal.

A voice from not more than a yard away carried above the cheering of the onlookers. 'Tell me, son, are you thinkin' of takin' up bronco bustin'?'

Billy turned to find his father sitting the buckboard on the outside of the fence. He managed a grin and a shake of the head.

'Not professionally, Pa, but it sure is a fine kind of sport for an amateur. How come you sneaked up on me like this? If I'd known you were comin' to the Wales' place I'd have waited until you arrived!'

The Reverend Harry Bartram gave a deep baritone laugh, and his obvious good humour did much to put Rancher Wales and the others at ease. They clustered round the preacher, glancing from him to his son, perched on high, and back again.

Billy had not acquired his father's colouring. The Reverend was a tall, heavy man in his early fifties with crisp, dark, wavy hair. His full face was cleanshaven, although his chin was already acquiring the bluish sheen of men whose beard was really black.

The fresh-complexioned face and grey eyes radiated energy and good humour, and issued a challenge to the world. He was a very positive personality which a neat flat black hat, a jacket of the same colour, and a clerical collar failed to neutralise.

'I can see you want to be a doer of deeds, as well as a writer of the facts, a chronicler of others' deeds,' the preacher remarked.

Before Billy could reply, the Wales family chipped in with their congratulations for a very promising piece of riding. While they talked Billy scrambled down the poles and joined his father on the buckboard, which turned slowly and gradually made its way to the ranch house situated a furlong away.

The Bartrams, father and son, took coffee on the house gallery, along with Norm and his two sons, his wife and one of the daughters-in-law. It was a nice little get-together, with an exchange of information and a great showing of mutual respect.

No one ever suggested a time for leaving when the preacher visited. On this particular occasion, Mrs Wales Senior looked a trifle disappointed when he stood up, stretched his long legs and explained that his pressing duties required him to move on.

At this, all parties rose to their feet and tentative enquiries were made as to when the Reverend could be expected in the evening for a good meal. Bartram Senior answered simply and diplomatically, and thanked them warmly as he went back to his conveyance.

Billy perceived that his father wanted

him to ride along with him and converse. Billy's horse, a spirited dun, was tethered to the rear of the buckboard, while the young man joined the other on the box. To the sounds of a magnificent vocal send-off, the two horses carried the vehicle and the two travellers away from Box W land.

'I've never seen you take on a horse with the temper of that one before, son,' the Reverend observed, when they were beyond earshot.

'I don't suppose you have, Pa, but a young man in these parts has to show some aptitude with horses if his contemporaries ain't goin' to think him soft. I didn't think I did too badly.'

'Oh, you didn't, lad, but it sure is a risky business. After all, if you'd broken a bone or two the *Cochise Creek Chronicle* might be short of a good reporter at the end of your holiday.'

Billy whistled. 'Yes, I see what you mean, Pa. But all I've collected are a few bruises, so we don't need to contemplate that sort of setback. What sort of a day did you have?'

The time was late afternoon, and the Reverend had been away from home since mid-morning. Billy, taking a long holiday from his job over in Cochise Creek, Arizona, had been away the night before, sleeping out at a ranch beyond the Box W.

'Oh, pretty good, son. Pretty good. I visited three homes. Two homesteads and a small ranch. All seemed to be workin' hard, an' likely to succeed. One family wanted help, but it was the kind a medical man provides rather than a preacher. An oldish woman with a bad disease, but her faith was strong enough.

'So here I am, headin' back home-wards, an' wonderin' if I should go on a little further tonight, so as to visit the nesters up the south side of the big creek.'

Billy, who knew his widower father's habits as well as most, nodded. 'Anybody stayin' with us right now?'

The Reverend raised his brows.

'Why, yes, son. A young woman happened along yesterday. In her own conveyance. A Mrs Della Rhodes, a young widow from further east. She'll be at the house now. She made no mention of movin' on when I left her.'

'Does she have any special reason for travellin' the country, Pa?'

The young man's interest was instantaneous. His father noted this, but the older man's face looked rather grave as he brooded over the matter. The Reverend continued to stare, until Billy coughed and broke in upon his thoughts.

'She says she's lookin' for her younger brother, Billy.'

'Do you have any reason to doubt her, Pa?'

The Reverend shrugged. 'No, no reason at all, son. But she's so desperate to find him it makes me wonder about her. She's a personable young woman, as you'll see. I wonder what you'd do if you were placed in the same dilemma as *I* am.'

'What dilemma is that, Pa?' Billy asked patiently.

'Well, I'll tell you. This young man, name of Sandy East, came through our part of the county on his way towards the west. I took quite a fancy to him, as a matter of fact. But when he moved on, one of the things he asked was that I shouldn't tell anyone where he had gone.'

'But his own sister, surely that's different, Pa?' Billy protested, gesturing wildly with his hands.

'His sister is still 'anyone', so it seems to me,' the Reverend argued back.

And the discussion did not go much further. When asked if he thought the young woman ought to be told where young Sandy had gone next, Billy replied that it depended upon the secret-sharer's summing up of the parties concerned. The preacher was surprised at the answer, but he made due note of it, and parted with his son as the trail approached the small island on which the Bartrams had their home.

It was a warm, easy parting. The older man drove his conveyance on in the same direction, while Billy — having transferred himself to the dun — crossed the wooden bridge on to the southern side of the wooded island which nestled in the middle of Big Creek.

★　★　★

The island was a hundred yards wide and several hundred yards long. Billy had used the only bridge to get there. The channel on the north side, however, could be negotiated by a comparatively shallow ford. Along the backbone of the island a series of small hollows alternated with lush rounded mounds. Scrub pine and oak trees grew in abundance, so that the three buildings built along the length of the island were hidden from one another by spreading foliage.

At the eastern end of the island was the log cabin which served as the home of Jabez and Jessie Pool, a negro and his wife, in their fifties. Jabez, a sparely built fellow with close-cropped grey hair, acted as the unofficial caretaker of the island, while Jessie, a very plump, good-natured woman with boundless energy, did the duties of housekeeper to the reverend gentleman when necessary.

The other two buildings consisted of the Bartram house and the stable nearby. These were very much nearer the western end of the island and opposite the ford on the north side.

As the dun's shoes hit the soil of the island, Billy became more aware of his bruises, and, not wanting to meet a visiting female in his present condition, he gave the buildings a miss, riding across the island and heading his mount into a small inlet opposite the bridge, where he had bathed for years, before leaving home.

A cursory glance was sufficient to show that there was no one about. He stripped off his gun belt, and discarded his hat and boots before diving into the creek to cool himself off. The action of the tepid water on his body refreshed him. He broke surface, tossed his head, sucked in air and swam towards the north in a fast crawl.

Having tired himself a little, he turned on his back, and contemplated the cloudless sky above him. While the blue expanse occupied his eyes, his thoughts went back to the subject which he had discussed with his father. He recollected the name of the youthful visitor, who had taken the preacher's fancy. Sandy East was a name he had heard before. In some way it was connected with his livelihood, his being a deputy sheriff over the territorial line.

A great many of the names which a peace officer memorised tended to be those of law-breakers. Billy found himself mentally ticking off names and pictures on recent reward notices. He felt certain that he was on the right lines in considering 'wanted' men, but the name of Sandy East remained a mystery.

The failure of his memory rather

depressed him. And this sent his thoughts over to another matter. Since his last visit home, he had left his job as a reporter on the *Cochise Creek Chronicle* and taken to wearing a peace officer's badge as a deputy sheriff. Somehow, he had not got round to telling his father of the change. He was afraid, he supposed, that the preacher would not approve of his being a peace officer.

After brooding over his lack of frankness, he made for the shore, swimming with a slow, economic breast-stroke. He stripped off, laid out his clothes to dry, and sat with his knees drawn up in a thinker's attitude until a pleasant musical sound drifted to him from the direction of his home.

Although the house was not visible from where he was, he glanced in the direction of it. Someone was playing the upright piano, and playing it well. The preacher played a tune or two, now and again, but the late Mrs Bartram had been the real musician in the family.

Billy surmised that the piano had not

been played as well since his mother's death. Someone with a nice feel for Austrian piano concertos was really giving the instrument an airing. Obviously, it had to be the young female visitor, the sister of Sandy East. He wondered if the widowed sister looked as attractive as her music sounded.

Quite intrigued by this time, he dressed himself again, collected the dun and walked slowly in the direction of the house. He was holding the horse in the last cluster of trees when the music stopped as abruptly as it had started.

Billy was puzzled. He dismounted, and walked the dun as far as the stable, leaving it hitched to the rail outside. He walked the few remaining yards past the stable and edged on tiptoe towards the big living-room, where the piano was situated.

He did not make a habit of creeping up on people, and he felt a little guilty as he paused just outside the window and peered in. Almost at once, he spotted the young visitor. She was rather under the average height for a girl, and apparently in her late twenties. Her copper-coloured hair was worn long, and pinned on this occasion on the top of her head. Her eyes were blue, and the green gown she was wearing made her look very shapely.

Billy was most surprised; not by the young woman's appearance, but by her behaviour. She had left the vicinity of the piano, and was busy at the preacher's desk, rapidly pulling out one item after another, as though searching for something.

The onlooker remained hidden. Tiring of searching the desk, Della Rhodes gave her attention to the bookshelf which stretched from floor to ceiling at the wall behind the desk. With complete disregard for any other consideration, the guest started to pull out books and shake them, as though secret messages might be concealed between their pages. After about a minute of silent observation, Billy withdrew as quietly as he had arrived.

Another half hour went by before he approached the house again in the company of Jessie Pool. The incident was not mentioned.

2

The meal which Jessie prepared for the evening was a good one. Della Rhodes concentrated upon a show of good manners at first, and then gradually allowed her personality to sparkle. Prompted by Billy, she played the piano some more, after the meal.

Around nine o'clock, Jabez came along to collect his wife. The Pools kept early hours, and as soon as the old negro appeared, Billy made an excuse to break up the gathering. He explained that there was a separate bed made up in the loft over the stable, for occasions like these when a lady was staying as a guest unchaperoned.

Della protested at having to put him out of his own home, but he insisted on going to the stable, and that settled the affair. The guest was left with the run of the house, and she turned in about a half hour after the other three had gone. Of the preacher, there was no sign, but Billy was used to his being away, because the Reverend Bartram was forever extending the boundaries of his parish.

Della had the breakfast meal started when Jessie came around and she showed herself to be thoroughly at home in a kitchen. They ate well, and then discussed the future.

'Tell me, Billy, will your father expect me to move on while he is away?' Della asked, as she pushed away her food plate.

'You come and go as you wish, Della. If Pa said for you to use this house, then he meant it. I guess he'd be disappointed, though, if you resumed your journey without seeing him again. So why don't you hang on till he comes back? Me, I'm thinking of takin' a ride into Indian Springs today to look up one or two old friends. If you wanted, we could go along together, an' you could do a bit of window shoppin' in

21

the town. What do you say?'

'Oh yes, I think I'd like that, Billy,' the young woman enthused. 'How soon can we start?'

Twenty minutes later, the short ride into town, which was south-east of the Bartram home, was taken. Della Rhodes had changed her clothing for a cream shirt and denims, the better to be able to ride the roan mare, on loan from the Bartram stable. She had tied back her long hair under a big-brimmed hat which was not unlike a Confederacy campaign hat, and as soon as they approached the settlement her attractiveness began to draw the eyes of men and women alike.

They dismounted near the first block of shops. After taking coffee together, they parted by mutual arrangement, one to shop and the other to move around and visit friends.

Billy knew many people, but he was drinking beer in the Wagon Wheel, on his own, when he saw a man's face which he thought ought to be familiar to him. The other man was also alone, and when he perceived Billy's interest in him, he retired to an empty table with his beer glass and thoughtfully returned his gaze.

The fellow in question had a seasoned red face, black brows, a thin, short moustache and a cleft chin. In age, he was about thirty-six. After a time, he rose to his feet again and walked towards Billy, who showed mild surprise.

'Howdy, mister, I saw you were interested in me. The name's Nils Raymore. I'm a stranger jest passin' through. Have we met before, by any chance?'

Billy grinned. 'Well now, I don't rightly know. When I first saw your face I thought it was familiar, but I don't know the name, an' I'm beginnin' to doubt my memory for faces now. Maybe you have a double, huh?'

Raymore swirled beer round his mouth and pretended an interest in this supposition, but obviously the idea of a double did not please him.

'By the way, I'm Billy Bartram. I was raised in these parts, an' right now I'm moochin' around, lookin' up old friends. Will you have a beer with me?'

Surprisingly, Raymore refused, claiming that he had a prior engagement. Billy watched him leave the saloon, and shook his head, forgetting about the encounter, for a time.

★ ★ ★

In the next few hours, Billy engaged in a horseshoe tossing contest at the back of the smithy. He also had himself a good midday meal, and followed that with a siesta. He met so many people that the time did not drag. Della Rhodes was forgotten, for the time being, when the young man left the barber's shop in the early evening and returned to the Wagon Wheel to drink more beer.

A man barged against him as he went through the batwing doors, but there was no altercation. One glass of beer had slaked Billy's thirst when a small boy of the town pushed up against him and said that a man wanted to talk to him up the street.

'All right, lad, if he can't come in here to talk, then I'll have to go out and find him. Lead the way, amigo.'

Out they went, Indian fashion. To Billy's surprise the journey was almost non-existent. 'He's waitin' for you up the alley, so if it's all right, I'd like to take my quarter now. I have other things to do.'

Billy glanced down at the young urchin in the straw hat. He was sincere enough. A two-bit piece changed hands and the youngster scampered away before the young peace officer had the chance to investigate the matter of the rendezvous.

He was thinking that if the man who wanted to speak to him was as near as the alley beside the saloon, then he could just as easily have come into the saloon and delivered his own message.

Shrugging, Billy stepped into the alley and looked for the other party. At first he appeared not to be there. Four huge trash cans and some small boxes were all the items to be seen. Deeply puzzled, Billy walked up the alley. He was taken by surprise when a figure rose up between the two trash cans, and a large hairy hand gripped his bandanna.

Breath charged with whisky hit him in the face. 'I've been waiting for you, Bartram. I didn't like the looks you were givin' me this mornin'. You ain't kiddin' me, either. All that talk about me havin' a double, too! The name is still Raymore, only I'm goin' to teach you a lesson, see?'

Billy gasped. 'Raymore? I haven't given you a thought since I offered you beer this morning. Back off, will you? You've got the wrong impression. I have this interest in people's faces, that's all. It doesn't do anybody any harm.'

Even as he made this excuse, Billy knew that he was not telling the whole truth. His training as a peace officer was largely to blame for his fascination with faces.

'One of the first things a Western gent has to learn is not to be nosey about another man's past, Bartram. I'm surprised you didn't know that!'

Raymore was talking quite coherently, even if he had drunk a lot of liquor. Billy was about to protest again when the accuser released his bandanna and hit him a swinging blow across the mouth. The time for soothing remarks was over.

The fair young man backed off. He dodged two swinging blows, but a third right-hander caught him on the angle of his jaw. Nor was this to be all defence. He dropped into a prize-fighter's crouch then, and fought back, missing once before he connected with Raymore's ribs.

The latter was stocky and sinewy. He had the build of a miner, or someone used to heavy physical work. At the rear end of the alley, the two men traded punches. Billy's work improved as his eyes adjusted to the shadows in the passage. Dust came up as they shifted their feet.

At the end of three minutes, Billy began to slip more punches. He threw about half as many and connected with most. Raymore crouched for better protection. After another bout of punch trading he came in fast. A short right connected with his chest, and slowed him sufficiently for Billy to dodge out of his way.

Raymore blundered on, hit the fence and received two stinging blows in the face as he turned around. He blinked slowly, and failed to come forward again. Gradually, his knees buckled and he slid down the wall. He stuck out a hand, but this only saved his face as his trunk canted over in the dirt.

Billy walked slowly away and rested his weight on the nearest trash can, while his lungs brought him back to normal. By the time he was ready to move on, Raymore had not moved.

Billy glanced back at him and decided to leave him. The aggressor could recover in his own good time.

★　★　★

By the time the young peace officer had cleaned himself up and taken a stroll to sort out his thoughts the time was approaching eight o'clock. He felt that Della Rhodes would certainly have left town for the Bartram home.

The fist fight had temporarily killed some of the geniality in Billy. His face was not badly marked, but he felt that he did not want to make polite conversation over the evening meal, so he saddled up and made the return trip at a steady pace.

He crossed the bridge on to the island without hesitation, but instead of heading directly for the Bartram end, he turned towards the east spot where the Pools had their cabin. Big Jessie, who had been on the point of leaving for the Bartram house to deal with the evening meal, raised her plump arms in mock surprise.

'Why, Master Billy, ain't you goin' along home to take dinner with your Pa's visitin' young lady? Your Pa ain't back at all, an' I felt sure you'd want to keep her company!'

Billy grinned and swung to the ground. 'No, I ain't goin' along home to take the meal with her, Jessie. I've had a busy day, an' right now I want a light picnic meal, because I'm figurin' on doin' some fishin' on the south side. Do you think you could fix me up?'

Chuckling to herself, the negress went indoors, knowing that Billy would follow her. In a few minutes, she had made sandwiches and filled a bottle with a cool, thirst-quenching beverage. Billy's fishing gear had been at the Pools' house since the last time he used it. He collected everything he needed, and walked towards the south side of the island, leaving the horse for Jabez to look after.

Soon, he was established at his

favourite fishing spot between weeping willows some fifty yards away from the Bartram house and stable. As the trees behind him swayed, he had a brief glimpse of lamplight coming from the house, but this time no one was playing the piano.

*   *   *

In the next hour, Billy caught four small fish. He felt pleased with himself. He had eaten all his packed food and most of the beverage had gone, too. He was wondering whether he should make this a long session, seeing that he had run out of daylight, or whether he ought to return to the barn and turn in early.

A half hour after dusk, the sounds of a horse being led across the bridge alerted him. He had filled his lungs to yell out a query as to who it was when instinct alone prevented the call. He shrugged in the darkness. Whoever it was, he would know soon enough the identity of the caller.

He turned again to his fishing, but the advent of the newcomer had broken his interest in the sport. He leaned back and listened, while the led horse was tethered somewhere on the island side of the bridge. This was unusual. He wondered what it could mean.

Within minutes he became aware that the newcomer was heading for the Bartram place, rather than the Pool home. Moreover, precautions were being taken about noise. The stranger's progress was now scarcely perceptible.

Moved by curiosity, Billy secured his rod and began to crawl away from the creek bank, so that he would be close enough to witness the arrival of the stealthy caller. A single tree bole hid him as the shadowy figure of a man negotiated the stable and stepped towards the rear gallery of the house.

Just clear of the lamplight which spilled from the rear windows, the stranger hesitated, looking around and using his ears to advantage. At length, he appeared to feel justified in approaching the house. He tiptoed up on to the gallery and tapped lightly on the outer door.

A shadow moved and grew still beyond the curtains, showing that Della was on the alert. Billy waited, wondering how she would handle the situation, and whether she was in any danger. It was only when the door opened, letting out more light, that he had his first inkling of the newcomer's identity.

Della gasped and lowered the lamp she carried.

'Nils? Nils, is that you?'

Her voice was muted, but it carried. Nils Raymore murmured something in return. He shrugged his shoulders, aware of Mrs Rhodes' displeasure but doggedly refused to withdraw.

'You fool!' she gasped hoarsely. 'Didn't we decide that you would stay right away from me durin' the time I was enjoyin' the preacher's hospitality? An' now you're here, an' as large as life! What would you have done if the

Reverend had opened the door himself?'

'As like as not ask for a drink, an' then leave. But the parson ain't here, Della, so cool down. I met a man today, an' I thought I ought to tell you about him, see?'

'The preacher's son could come ridin' back here at any moment an' then I'd have a whole lot of difficult explainin' to do, seein' as I'm supposed to be travellin' alone on a private matter.'

'It was the preacher's son I wanted to tell you about, Della!'

The young woman showed surprise. 'It looks as if Billy Bartram talked to you with his fists. You'd better come on in, but you can't stay more than a few minutes, you understand!'

Raymore removed his hat and stepped into the house. The door was closed again, and on this occasion Della pulled net drapes to give her greater privacy during her visitor's stay.

Billy stayed where he was for ten

minutes. Obviously Della Rhodes was in no danger from the fellow. But it was a surprise, Raymore turning up in that stealthy fashion! If the young peace officer had drawn the right conclusion, then the widow had a male accomplice making the rounds with her.

As he withdrew, Billy reflected that this revelation would probably not surprise his father.

3

Billy and Della met again at breakfast. Della explained how she had grown tired of the town atmosphere in the afternoon, and made her way back with one or two purchases. Billy claimed to have had rather a lot to drink, and, consequently, he had been late returning to the island.

No mention was made of the surreptitious visitor, nor was the identity of the man with whom Billy had fought revealed. Della suggested that she might resume her journey in search of her restless young brother late in the day, so long as she did not miss the preacher altogether and thus deny herself the pleasure of thanking him for his hospitality.

After breakfast, Della washed some clothes while Billy went away to do some more fishing. He had a feeling that his father would return before midday, and he wanted to be on hand for an early meeting.

It was around eleven in the morning that the hardworked buckboard showed up on the trail from the south-west. Billy saw it in the distance. He lined his spyglass on it and confirmed his father's approach. After that, he acted more positively, rounding up the dun and putting the saddle on its back for a hurried getaway.

Within five minutes the hooves of the dun were ringing on the bridge timbers. On the south bank, at a distance of perhaps a quarter of a mile, father and son came together. The preacher noted a certain excitement in his son's face, as well as faint marks which suggested a fight.

'Well met, son, an' what makes you come hurryin' all this way to meet a dull fellow like myself?'

Billy grinned and moved the dun into line beside the buckboard.

He said: 'I wanted to talk to you before you got back on the island.'

'All right, son, I'm listening.'

Thus prompted, Billy began. 'You remember we talked about whether a sister should be told her brother's whereabouts when he's asked that they should be kept a secret?'

The Reverend nodded and frowned against the sun.

'I don't think Mrs Della Rhodes ought to be given that information, Pa. I wanted you to know my views before you arrived in the young woman's presence. She may not be workin' in the brother's best interests.'

'Well now, there's a point of view for you. Do you mind tellin' me how you came to formulate this attitude? Obviously, Della Rhodes is no longer a stranger to you. Have you quarrelled?'

Billy shook his head. He launched into his explanation, starting with the time when he had witnessed the young woman searching the desk and the bookshelves. The preacher was most interested to hear about the episode, but in no way perturbed. Billy resumed with a description of the visit to town, the exchanges with Nils Raymore who did not like to be looked upon, and the fist fight in the alley, later in the day.

'Is there more?' the preacher asked.

'There is,' Billy assured him. 'After dark the same man slipped on to the island. He was almost at the house before I identified him. But he wasn't lookin' for me. He came to contact Mrs Rhodes, and what's more he knew her well. I got the impression that they were travellin' together!'

Buckboard and dun horse were checked at the approaches to the bridge. 'Did you have the impression you'd seen the man Raymore in some other place, Billy? On a reward notice, for instance, or somewhere like that?'

Billy was startled. He glanced at his father and saw that the preacher already knew about his being a peace officer. He nodded.

The Reverend went on: 'I've met a lot of peace officers in my time, and I can usually tell, son. Don't think I altogether disapprove of your change of employment. It all depends on how you use your authority, and what you do with the weapons you carry. Why did you become a peace officer?'

'There was a man I admired, a county sheriff named Hartley Timms, Pa. He was drawn away from his men and deliberately gunned down by an outfit actin' under the orders of Long John Carrick. No one was ever brought to justice for the crime, and that was what made me want to try my hand as a peace officer.'

Half a minute of unbroken silence built up between them.

'Have you thought more about this man's face?'

'I still don't know why I think I know him, Pa. I think he's on the wrong side of the law, or pretty close to it. Maybe you could enlighten me about that young brother, Sandy East.'

The Reverend swung to the ground, lit his pipe and leaned over the bridge rail while he prepared to explain certain things.

'About three or four years ago, Sandy East was one of two no-good youngsters known as the Coyote Kids. He's around twenty-one now, so he must have been teamed up with Red Murdo, the other boy, when he was seventeen or eighteen.

'Sandy had some kin, and Red was an orphan. Anyway, they got into a lot of scrapes after workin' with one or two big cattle outfits, an' then it was rumoured they were running with one of Long John Carrick's gangs. Jest how much real law-breakin' they ever did is not clearly known. Maybe they did a little rustlin' and a few small jobs with the adult outlaws, but they weren't trusted, and the time came when they were chased off.

'I believe they happened upon some valuables, which they kept for themselves and then reburied. Sandy says Red was taken ill, and then they split up, around the time when Long John was put away for a year or two on a minor charge.

'Sandy went back to Texas, where he

was born, and kept out of trouble for quite a time, but Red appears not to have been able to settle. He remained in southern Arizona for a time, maybe he's still there. Anyhow, he's in trouble now, and young Sandy is going to try and help him.

'I've got an awful feelin' that circumstances are goin' to put that boy back on the wrong side of the law. So I'm sayin' this, son. If you do happen to bump into Sandy East, give him a break. There's a lot of good in him, an' maybe his friend is the same way, too.'

Billy put a match to a thin, home-rolled cigarette. 'It's an interestin' story, Pa, an' I wouldn't hesitate to help Sandy, given the opportunity. Jest so long as it doesn't involve helping Long John's sadistic outlaws. Hearin' all this has made me restless. I think I'll start back for the territorial line later in the day. I take it you won't tell Della anything which will lead her to Sandy?'

Talking round his pipe, the Reverend explained: 'I never did know where

Sandy went after he left here. So there's no fear of my letting him down. As for you, I think you're right to get movin' if you feel restless. If you don't want to go right on back to your job, there's a friend you could look up about a day's ride away from here.

'Name of Paul Gatling, a trapper, who graduated this way from Canada. He'd be glad to meet anyone as keen on fishin' as you are. I'll explain to you how to find the place, if you like.'

'Sure, I'd like to know the details, Pa, but before you tell me, answer me this. How long is it since Sandy East left your house?'

'That's an easy one, son. Jest about a week is all. Seven or eight days. Now, about the route to Gatling's place . . . '

* * *

The Bartrams, father and son, shared the midday meal with Della Rhodes, who was in her most charming and talkative mood. Billy made an effort and managed to take his leave of the others at an hour when they were wondering whether to fight off the heat, or succumb to a siesta.

He left by the ford. His father watched and waved across the narrow strip of water, and then went off to talk to Jabez Pool about one or two pressing small matters. Around mid-afternoon, Della visited the Pool house and made it clear that she was preparing to leave the Bartram house within the hour.

Jessie helped with the packing and Jabez saw to the lightweight wagon and the horses. Around five in the evening, the vehicle rolled across the bridge and turned westward, prior to finding a route towards the southwest. Della was profuse in her thanks for the hospitality shown to her, but her determination to get a move on showed in her actions and the way she talked.

The Reverend Bartram gave her a last wave, and crossed the bridge again alone. He was in a deeply thoughtful mood. He was wondering if his son would meet up with Sandy East, and whether the determined sister would succeed in locating her elusive brother.

★ ★ ★

Around seven that same evening, Billy found himself a camping spot near a dried-out arroyo which had water just a few inches below the centre of its bed. He made himself comfortable, built a fire and spread his roll beside it, full of the revelations of his father and the fascinating but unfinished story of the Coyote Kids.

One thing which Billy had kept from his father was the fact that Long John Carrick was about to be released from the Yuma Penitentiary in Arizona almost at any time. The return of this diehard renegade to the scene of his former crimes could start another wave of violence in southern Arizona. It could also have a bearing upon the affairs of the Coyote Kids.

Uppermost in Billy's mind as he

drifted off to sleep were two consider-
ations. One, to try and help Sandy East,
if at all possible. And two, to have a
healthy crack at Long John and his
renegade followers before they became
too united again and thoroughly steeped
in crime.

★   ★   ★

The sun awakened the lone traveller at
a reasonable hour. For once, however,
he was content to lie back and sip water
from his canteen. For a full half hour he
lazed, listening to the small animals and
birds moving around in the nearby
scrub.

In the far distance, a few points north
of west, was a gap in a low range of
hills. That gap was the landmark he was
making for, the key to the valley in
which Paul Gatling, the former trapper,
lived in remote splendour with nature.
He screwed up his eyes the better to see
it and saw a large white bird glide
through the pass on slowly flapping

wings. The sight of it made him restless again.

He rose to his feet, prowled the dry creek bed, kicked some life into the fire embers and scrambled out in the direction of a scrub pine. Soon, he was climbing the tree for a better view of his route. On a swaying branch, he studied it distantly, not feeling any special excitement until he turned in the other direction and examined the terrain over which he had travelled.

It was wild, lonely land, but he was not alone upon it. The sight of a distant wagon made him catch his breath. Moreover, there was something about the colour of the canvas awning which made him think that life in the near future was likely to be far from dull.

The awning was a rather unusual tint of pale green. Most canvas awnings of that colour rapidly became faded in the sun. This one had not. It was either the one he had seen parked beside the Bartram stable or an identical article. And this latter consideration seemed unlikely because there were two people sitting up front on the wagon, a man and a woman.

He had neglected to bring his glass with him on the climb, but he felt reasonably sure that he was seeing Della Rhodes and Nils Raymore. And that had to mean they were following him. They had changed their route quite considerably, probably in the belief that he — Billy — knew where to locate Sandy East.

As he climbed down again, Billy gave a wry smile. Maybe they were all on the wrong route.

4

After that, breakfast was a hurried affair. All the time Billy was eating his rashers, he was pacing about, wondering what was best to be done to try and throw off pursuit. He felt that he had to enter the valley where Gatling lived by the obvious route. Any other would take too long.

It became clear that one thing was in his favour. There was no established track for a cart to use over the terrain which lay ahead. If the wagon was not stopped altogether, it would at least be slowed down.

He gathered his few belongings together, attached them to the saddle and mounted up. The arroyo in which he had camped was his obvious route away from the place. Hidden in its depths he could make steady progress before the wagon got too close. A lot depended upon the direction of the stream bed, and how far it ran before it levelled out with the surrounding country.

Over the first furlong his confidence mounted. The arroyo was stretching out before him in a steady arc. At first he was heading north, but after that the direction gradually changed further and further westward, until he was facing in the direction of the gap in the hills.

Perhaps two hundred yards went by towards the west before the first trickle of water began to show, and then the trickle broadened and became a little deeper. Billy stayed in the water and only broke out from the gorge when it changed direction again towards the east.

On firmer, higher ground, he dismounted long enough to obliterate the marks he had made while emerging from the stream. After that, he pushed the hard-working dun to a useful pace which gradually took care of the miles between the stream and the hills. By the middle of the morning, the animal was toiling up the last furlong before the pass.

A light fresh breeze blew through the gap. Horse and man recovered their breath in it and shortly afterwards Billy called a short halt. He rested long enough to give his mount a rough grooming besides rocking the saddle and providing a drink of water.

*   *   *

The sun was past its zenith when the sweating horse worked its way down a winding path which came from the slopes of the hills. Sun rays were reflected upon a flat stretch of water on lower ground and the verdure improved quite perceptibly.

The stream in the valley linked the lowest points of several grass-grown hollows. In one of them which was well to westward the log cabin home of Paul Gatling, trapper and hermit, was located.

As Billy approached the building through the last stand of timber, he perceived the occupant, who had just emerged from the doorway. The newcomer waved at once. His greeting was acknowledged, though without any undue enthusiasm.

Billy studied this man who had to be his father's friend. He saw a man of about five-feet seven-inches in height wearing a coonskin cap on his head, and a plaid coat buttoned over a dun shirt. The complexion was dark, weathered no doubt by long hours spent in the open air.

About ten yards separated them when Billy called out: 'Howdy, friend, you must be Paul Gatling! I'm Billy Bartram, the son of the Reverend Bartram from Indian Springs way. Pa suggested I should call on you, as I was returning in this direction to my place of work. Sure you don't mind me invadin' your valley?'

The rather severe expression on the trapper's face suddenly gave way to an expansive smile. Gold-filled teeth were revealed. At the same time, the long-barrelled hunting rifle was lowered to the ground.

'Any friend of the Reverend Bartram is a friend of mine. Especially the preacher's son. Right now, I'm startin' out to examine some traps on the other side of the water. I'd ask you to come along with me, but you'll be tired after your long ride. Perhaps you'd rather stay around the cabin till I get back. What do you say?'

Billy grinned easily. 'The thing I'd like best is to take a swim in the stream, while you're busy. How would that be, Paul?'

'If that's what you want, Billy, then that's the thing to do. Why don't you turn the dun loose an' leave him to forage for himself? He'll find food and drink without difficulty. Meantime, I'll show you the best spot to bathe before I cross over the other side.'

Billy was whistling as he gave the dun its freedom. He stacked his gear against the wall of the cabin and hurriedly joined Gatling, who was standing between two trees waiting for him. They fell into step and gradually moved towards the water.

'Sure is quiet around here, except for the sounds of nature,' Billy remarked.

'A man who likes the company of his fellows wouldn't come out an' live in this neck of the woods,' Gatling replied, with a shrug.

The trapper strolled along, moving easily on muscular limbs. Billy glanced at him from time to time, and was surprised to see that tiny globules of perspiration had formed on his upper lip. The plaid coat and the coonskin hat looked to be warm gear for the heat of the day.

'Ain't you a little on the warm side, Paul, wearin' thick clothes on a day like this?'

The trapper's nostrils flared. 'A man wears what he is used to.'

Billy broke a short silence, knowing that he was dealing with a man who was touchy about his appearance. 'I've been meaning to ask you ever since we met, Paul. Have you had a visitor around here in the past few days? A young red-headed fellow about twenty-one years of age?'

Gatling was slowly shaking his head, but Billy went on.

'Answers to the name of Sandy East, on account of his hair colouring. I thought I'd ask because he stayed with my Pa for a while, and Pa thought he might call on you. Still, if you ain't seen him there's no use in goin' on talkin' about him is there?'

The trapper smiled again. 'This valley is very quiet, Billy. Not many men come through this way. Why, at this time I don't even have a dog for company.'

A walk of five minutes, during which they discussed the merits and demerits of keeping tame animals in remote cabins, brought them to the side of the stream. Here and there a slight ripple showed the presence of fish. Billy remarked that Paul's diet was probably a very varied one, and that suggestion was popular.

Gatling talked at some length about the different sorts of food which found their way into his diet, and then they were nearing the small inlet where the light birchbark canoe was drawn up.

'This is my transport for crossin' the stream, Billy, an' I'd recommend you to swim near this point. If you want fairly shallow water keep to the left. Further right, it's definitely deeper — by several feet.'

Billy walked around the canoe admiring the workmanship which had gone into the making of it. Gatling accepted the praise, though he claimed not to be an expert in canoe-making. A sudden impatience seemed to take hold of him. He glanced into the sky in various directions and laid a hand on the canoe, anxious to be in it and across the water.

The newcomer bent his back and heaved it into the water, while the owner put aside his shoulder weapon and took up the double-ended paddle. Clear water lapped round the bows as Billy straightened up on the water's edge.

'Hope your traps are full, Paul!'

Gatling signalled with the paddle and dug it into the water, cutting across the current which had some power in it. 'I'll be back in an hour or so, Billy! If you get hungry, go back an' help yourself! The food ain't hard to find!'

'Adios, Paul. Don't hurry back on my account!'

Billy's parting words were muffled because he was pulling his shirt over his head as he said them. Off came his hat, his boots and his gun belt. Stripped to his denims, he moved about the bank, studying the water depth while Gatling rapidly gained the other shore.

The trapper took the boat inshore and ran up its length, leaping the bows and drawing it after him. The shoulder gun was back in his hand and he was ready to depart. This time, as he looked back, he merely gave a curt nod before heading towards the scrub and trees a few yards up the further slope.

Billy elected to go into the water on the deeper side of the inlet. As he straightened up his body for a dive, over a deep pool, he took time out to think that living out in the wilds had its drawbacks and compensations.

Swimming had always been a great joy to him, even from an early age. He saw it as the Westerner's best form of exercise, barring only horse riding. He raised his arms, holding them straight out from the shoulders, bent his legs and sprang forward, his body straightening and dipping by the head towards the cool, inviting waters.

His dive was a neat one. The whole of his body entered at surface level directly behind his arms, and the splash was not very marked. Down he went, savouring the sudden coolness, and watching the streams of bubbles which he had made bobbing about in the current and making their way back to the surface.

A darting silver fish went by. Some distance below him thin filmy green strands of moss undulated as the current pushed them. Billy thought again about Gatling and his warm clothing and the perspiration on his face, and then his lungs were bidding him get back to the surface.

He turned, jack-knifed his body and swam to the surface with powerful leg and arm movements. The colour of the water became lighter and lighter until his head broke the surface and he was turning on his back and sucking in the pure air.

When his lungs had been recharged, he rolled like a log and took notice of the way in which the current was pulling him across the tiny inlet. He lay on his back, content to let the current propel him for a time, while he studied the shapes of trees beautifully etched against the bright sky above them.

His thoughts went back to his reason for being where he was. Sandy East. Sandy had not taken the preacher's advice about calling on the trapper, which meant that he had gone west by an entirely different route. He — Billy — was still completely out of touch, and so was Della Rhodes and her male companion. Even if they found Gatling's home in the valley they would have made no progress.

This last conclusion brought a smile to his lips, but it did not linger there long. From the far bank came the crack of a shoulder gun, and a small missile no bigger than a rifle bullet ripped into the water within an inch of his chest. The sound it made was thoroughly disconcerting. It was a rifle bullet.

Billy rolled in the water, cast an anxious glance in the direction which Gatling had taken and at once perceived the trapper with his long gun to his shoulder, sighting for a second shot.

'Paul! What in tarnation . . . '

Billy failed to conclude his shouted protest. The man with the gun was bent upon his destruction and no amount of pleading would make him desist. A man swimming in water was certainly in a most invidious position when threatened by a gunman from dry land. He could not swim fast enough to save himself, nor could he afford to stay on the surface.

With his lungs half-filled, Billy ducked his head and swam downwards. For a time, his only thoughts were those connected with self-preservation. Three more bullets came ripping through the water perilously close just when he was thinking of surfacing again for fresh air. Without the air, there could be no survival. But surfacing was critically dangerous.

This time he went up at an angle, and when barely a foot of water remained above him, he stuck up his feet first in the hope that he would draw the sharpshooter's bullets away from his head and trunk. One of the two bullets which came at him grazed a toe nail, but otherwise no further damage was done.

Billy pushed up his face, rolled his

mouth and nose around for a few seconds, gulped in air and dropped from the surface again. Seconds slipped by before the next shot. He guessed that Gatling's weapon needed reloading. The waiting time lengthened and his lungs began to quake again. His imagination ran riot.

Was Gatling waiting for him to surface again? Was he to be destroyed when he came up again for breath? He knew several seconds of mental agony before he had to swim upwards again. This time he kicked out for the bank, hoping to encounter some overhanging shrub which might mask him.

The blood was pulsing through his head when he broke surface with the back of his head towards the trapper's back. Almost at once the shooting started again. A bullet came close to neck and shoulder. Oddly enough, he flinched but made no attempt to submerge. The gun shots seemed to have a double sound, almost as though they had an echo on the other bank.

Further gun discharges coaxed Billy's stunned brain towards the truth. Two guns were firing now. The men who held them were on opposite banks. Moreover, bullets were no longer landing in the water. The gunmen were firing at each other!

Billy had an ally from somewhere. As he glided under the outstretched drooping foliage of a weeping willow, he marvelled at this sudden change in his fortunes. His benefactor was out of sight, a few yards up the bank and partially hidden by trees, but Gatling was in view.

Even as the stunned swimmer peered at him the man in the coonskin cap received a bullet in the chest. He stepped back half a pace and went down on one knee, still trying to get his weapon back to his shoulder in order to reply.

More bullets, however, flew across the waterway fired by a skilled marksman. Another entered his chest and a third struck him in the head. Gatling toppled over backwards, released his weapon and the shooting which had started in so treacherous a fashion was over.

Unless the unknown had merely accounted for Gatling in order to give himself the privilege of killing a deputy sheriff.

5

Billy waited a minute, hearing only the sounds of nature once again. Even the birds seemed to have been quietened by the recent flurry of gunfire. The victor in the shoot-out made no attempt to move or to say anything and this had the effect of laying stress on the swimmer's nerves.

At last, he could stand the silence no longer. 'Hello, there!'

The unseen man coughed to clear his throat, while Billy held on to the flimsy hanging foliage above him, wondering if he should plunge back into deep water and head for the other shore.

'Who are you, an' why don't you show yourself?'

'Killin'. a man, even to save another man's life, don't come all that easy to me, mister. So have a little patience, will you? You're safe now.'

Another minute dragged by while Billy marvelled at this utterly sane explanation for the delay. After all, the fellow spoke the truth. An innocent man would have ended his days in the water but for the sudden appearance and prompt action of a totally unexpected stranger.

Slow footsteps came towards the trees which grew out of the bank. Feeling very vulnerable, Billy stepped clear of the masking foliage and stood waiting, his body dripping water.

The man who came towards him with the smoking gun had a youthful ingenuous appearance. He was about the average in height and built on spare, slim lines. His eyes were a deep blue and his mouth mobile. He wore a sheepskin vest over a check shirt. His stetson was dun-coloured, side-rolled and with the brim pointed in front. The face was cleanshaven. Crisp sandy hair showed in the tapering sideburns and at the nape of the neck where it crept into the bright green bandanna. The walking movements of the thighs caused the low-slung twin .45 Colt holsters to rock.

Lowering the muzzle of the Henry which had ended the shooting contest, he nodded and came to a halt a few feet away. 'The name is East. Sandy East. I'd be glad to know what name you go by in these parts.'

'Sandy East?' Billy blinked in surprise. 'But Gatling told me you hadn't been this way! I take it you've jest arrived?'

'No, I was along here a day or so ago. Left on a message, an' now I'm back again. You were sayin' something about Gatling jest then. And you didn't say your name.'

Sandy East stuck his thumbs through his belt and patiently waited to be enlightened.

'Billy Bartram, son of the preacher of the same name who lives near Indian Springs. I came here to see you rather than Gatling. The way *he* acted I'd be dead if if you hadn't come back right when you did. Can't think what came over him. An' anyways, he was supposed to be my Pa's friend. Why he would want to gun me down is a mystery.'

More relaxed now, East bent at the knees and squatted beside Billy, who looked him over some more.

'I take it you've never met Paul Gatling before today, Billy?'

'Nope, I never have. Wished I hadn't set eyes on him today, either. Can you throw any light on what's been happenin'?'

'That fellow over there with the coonskin cap on ain't Gatling. I have a picture of your Pa's friend right here in my pocket. Take a look at it an' you'll see the difference.'

East handed over a stiff card photograph. The look that went with it was troubled. Billy took it from him, his brain a surging turmoil of unrest and doubts. If Gatling had not welcomed him, then who had? The same question was going through the mind of the younger man.

The face in the picture was a striking one. It showed a man in his late forties with wise, all-seeing eyes and a goatee beard which seemed to lengthen a broad face. Billy glanced from the photograph to his deliverer and back again.

'I assure you, Billy, that's Paul Gatling. Right now, I'd like to get over the other side and see who it is who died wearing his coonskin cap and plaid jacket. That fellow wasn't here when I left, for sure.'

Billy was drying out, but he swung his arms to encourage better circulation. On an impulse he dived back into the water and began to swim across the creek. As his limbs worked for him, his thoughts were busy. Never in his remotest dreams had he expected to meet one of the Coyote Kids in circumstances such as these. No wonder the Reverend had taken to Sandy and suggested that there was much good in him.

The younger man waited while Billy scrambled out and moved up the other bank to examine the corpse. The man who had represented himself as Gatling was younger than the real man in years. His hair was darker and cropped fairly short over the crown. The tan on his face showed that he had never worn a beard, at least not for many months.

Blood from the chest had seeped into the plaid coat, but the head wound had scarcely disfigured him. Still full of the fellow's recent treachery, Billy dragged him and his weapon into the canoe and pushed off. East steered him in at the other side.

'I thought as much,' the sandy youth murmured, as he examined the corpse in close-up. 'Maurice Revere, or was it Devere? An old member of one of Long John's renegade groups. He must have been out in these parts lookin' for me. Right now it ain't healthy to be called East, or Murdo, for that matter.'

'Let's get him back to the cabin,' Billy suggested, 'then we can take a look for the real Gatling.'

East showed his approval by fetching

his horse to carry the burden, but his expression betrayed the fact that he expected Gatling to be dead.

Ten minutes later, Billy was dressed again. A brief search had failed to show any sign of the missing trapper, but there was a new mound of freshly dug soil in some trees at the rear of the dwelling. The two men took a hurried meal, and then turned to the new task, that of digging out the hole to find out what it contained.

The real Paul Gatling was in there, all right. He had two rifle bullets in his back, and his face wore a shocked expression put there by Maurice Devere's treachery.

'I say we leave Paul here, an' find another spot for Devere,' Sandy suggested.

'My sentiments exactly,' Billy agreed.

The body of Devere was weighted and tossed into the creek, where it sank to the bottom in deep water and came to rest. Back in the cabin, there was a lot to talk about.

'Let me talk first,' Billy suggested, when he had rolled smokes for both of them. 'I came here in the hope of meetin' you, so I hope you'll maybe be frank with me. I can tell you that your sister, Della Rhodes, has followed me part of the way here, along with a man who calls himself Nils Raymore. I had a fist fight with Raymore in Indian Springs. That doesn't mean he's all bad, but all the same he acts like he's on the wrong side of the law. Your sister is awful keen to catch up with you, an' you *do* have a sister, don't you?'

Sandy ran his fingers through his hair. 'Oh, sure, Della is my sister, all right. She has a lot of good in her, but in followin' me the way you tell it, with that Raymore in tow, I'd say she's out to try an' get rich quick at my expense, an' that ain't nice, even for a blood relation.'

'My Pa said you were ridin' to join your old pardner, Red Murdo, who's in some sort of trouble. Is that right?'

Sandy grinned. 'For a fellow who's

jest met up with me, you're askin' some mighty pertinent questions, Billy, but I guess it's okay if you're Reverend Bartram's son. Sure, Red is in trouble. We're both in trouble, but Red is the one nearest the Long John groups. They're tryin' to run him down on account of some old loot we stached away some time ago.

'Long John started his boys huntin' for us, even though he was still inside the pen himself. He sure has a lot of influence. Red managed to get word to me, so I'm goin' back to see if I can help him. The knowledge of where this loot is is a joint thing, shared by both of us, so I can't let him down, even if it means shootin' with guns all over again. What line of business are you in, Billy?'

'I'm a deputy sheriff over in Arizona territory, but that shouldn't worry you unduly. I was a newspaper man by trade. I only took to wearin' a badge because I wanted to see Long John out of the way for a sheriff's murder, an' his gangs broken up for all time. Besides, I promised my Pa I'd do anything I could to help you, an' I mean that.'

Sandy nodded and smiled briefly. 'Is my sister likely to be real close? I mean close enough to be in touch tonight, if we stay here?'

'It could happen,' Billy opined. 'But for havin' a wagon with her she could have been in this valley long before now. I reckon you and I ought to move on without delay. The point is, where do we make for?'

Sandy started to unbutton his shirt. He said: 'That Raymore hombre has a brother in cahoots with the Long John gangs. That's why he's a menace. Now, about the place to ride to. The main reason why I left here was to find someone with the latest information, newspaper wise, out of southern Arizona. I was lucky enough to find a traveller with jest the edition I wanted. It was last week's.'

He fished the folded paper out from his shirt, opened it out and handed it to Billy, who took it and studied it curiously. Among other items on the front was an article about the release of Long John Carrick from the penitentiary in Yuma. If the day was right, he had been a free man for two days, and could well be on his way towards Cochise County, which was where Billy worked.

'Was there anything else in here other than the news about Long John which took your fancy, Sandy?'

'Sure, a small item in the personal column. It says somebody has lost a sandy-haired mongrel dog with the initials C.K. on its collar. Any information to the office of the *Creek Chronicle*.'

'Are you the dog in question?'

'Sure, and the C.K. initials stand for 'Coyote Kid', as you've probably guessed. This is a lead to draw me to the right area. Red will give me a day or two to get into the area, an' then something will happen. He'll pull a stunt of some sort to show exactly where he is. Other folks may be a lot more subtle, but I think I'll get to him before any of our enemies do.'

Five minutes of silence built up between the two pensive men. They were alert for any approach to the cabin, but none came to disturb them. It was Billy who cleared his throat and spoke up first.

'If you trust me, I could get permission to ride along with you. At some time or another Long John and his boys will try to kidnap you, or make you see things their way. If I happened to be near, I'd have a wonderful opportunity to keep track of the gang. Besides, if there's any shootin' to be done, three guns are better than two. What do you think?'

Sandy was a lazy smoker. The smoke curled from his lips, which were not properly closed. He said: 'I think the heat will be on with a vengeance, now that Long John is free. We know exactly what he wants, an' he'll never let us alone until he gets it.

'If you think you could throw in with us, an' not be compromised as a peace officer, have a go, by all means. But you will be heading into big trouble. If Carrick's boys know how close you are to me, they'll hunt you the same as us. Your star won't protect you.'

Billy's thoughts went back to old Harvey Timms, the murdered sheriff, whose death had prompted him to take up his present work. He knew that Sandy was not exaggerating the dangers which lay ahead.

'I know that, Sandy, an' I'm prepared to take the risk. It's because of a bushwhacked sheriff that I wear a badge myself. Now, why don't you pack your gear and pull out in the next hour? I'll do my packin' a little more leisurely. If you're gone, and Della and her man see me, they'll come after me, an' I'll have a chance to put them on a false trail. Once I've lost them, I'll come back on the Cochise Creek trail as fast as I can.

'You'll be lookin' for Red, and I'll be lookin' for you. I feel sure we can make contact again before Long John gets too close. Maybe he'll be cautious for a while, seein' he's only jest out of prison.'

Young East stood up and paced the beaten earth floor with his hat pushed to the back of his head.

'All right, Billy, I'll go along with what you say. If an' when I meet up with Red, I'll tell him about you. If the renegades press us hard you might find yourself havin' to ride south of the border. Know what that means?'

Billy nodded and winked.

'One other thing, in seekin' to hoodwink Della and Raymore, be careful. Don't ever let Raymore draw a bead on you. Don't be fooled because his ugly face has not graced a reward dodger.'

Sandy thrust out his hand, and Billy rose to his feet and shook it. It was a strong, warm handshake marking the beginning of an eventful partnership. They wished each other well, and after that, young East's preparations took a mere five minutes. He mounted up on his rangy buckskin horse and walked it away from the cabin towards the west. Very soon, trees hid him from view.

Billy was left with a feeling of great loneliness, and a tendency to wonder how much time would elapse before he set eyes on Sandy East, the Coyote Kid, again. He had only known him for an hour, but it had been an eventful one, all sixty minutes of it.

6

As soon as Sandy East had departed, Billy made a tour of inspection from the back of his dun. In another hollow, not visited this far, he found two horses. One was a claybank and the other a skewbald. There was little to choose between them as regards performance and he did not spend a lot of thought on which belonged to Gatling and which to Devere.

He proposed to take them with him to the nearest settlement, a small town towards the south, known as Junction. In Junction, both horses could be sold and the money held over for any kin of Paul Gatling whom the local authorities managed to locate.

Before he left the valley, Billy found some traps on the other side of the water. He took along with him for early consumption a fat jackrabbit, and a couple of fresh fish. His last bit of observation was from near the top of a tree with the glass to his eye.

His pursuers had disappointed him in being this far behind. He could only conclude that the wagon had given some difficulty on the tortuous route up the arroyo and through the pass. Even while he was busy with the spyglass, the heads of the wagon's shaft horses came into view with Raymore behind them on the box, using the whip to get them over the high spot.

Billy smiled rather grimly, and slid back down the tree. He went back to the shack once more and settled himself at the table with pencil and paper. Red Murdo's message in the paper had given him an idea. He waved the pencil around in the air for a few moments, while his brow furrowed in thought.

Then he started to write:

Dear Paul,
I was sorry to miss you on my first visit to the valley where you live.

Time makes me move on again without waiting for your return. Pa sent his regards. Right now I have business in Junction, and after that something important will take me due south.

So long for now.

Billy Bartram.

Having written his faked message and pinned it to the table, Billy sat back and thought about it. He wondered how his father would feel when he heard about the happenings in Paul's valley. Paul murdered, and his murderer only just prevented from adding a second crime to his list.

Billy shuddered. The short hairs at the nape of his neck rose as he thought how he might be occupying a watery grave at that very moment. He swallowed hard as he glanced round the shelves, the rather primitive furniture, the worldly possessions of the dead man. There was nothing to be done with them, for the present. Any passing traveller could make use of the facilities, as was the custom.

Billy sighed, moved out and closed the door after him. He turned to the dun and swung into the saddle. Presently, he was moving at an economic pace across the hollows towards the south.

★　★　★

After sleeping out, the lone rider moved into the tiny settlement of Junction around ten in the morning. He talked with three men, the town marshal, the undertaker and principal storekeeper, and the stable owner. All three were known to his father, and that made taking them into his confidence an easy matter. The quartette took coffee together, while Billy's dun was getting light treatment from the ostler's man at the livery.

He explained what had happened at the Gatling cabin, and how he had left the note for a man who was already dead. The claybank and the skewbald were turned over to the liveryman, who felt sure that he could find a buyer for both in the near future.

The liveryman undertook to hand over to the storekeeper the proceeds of the sales, and all then promised Billy that they would give any enquirer (other than his father) the information that he had proceeded south in a hurry.

Having thus laid his plans, Billy topped up on food and drink and removed himself from the small town, first riding south and then doubling back towards the west.

★ ★ ★

Forty-eight hours later, Red Murdo, the other Coyote Kid, was stretched on his back in straw, taking his ease in a barn a few miles outside of Cochise Creek, in the first county over the boundary into Arizona territory.

The Kid was more homely than his 'old' riding partner. He had a small thin mouth, green half-squinted eyes, gapped teeth and a pointed jaw. He was an inch shorter and a year younger than Sandy. He wore an identical sheepskin vest to that of his friend, but the shirt under it was a faded blue colour, and the bandana at his neck was blue.

Murdo was smoking a home-rolled cigarette amid the straw with a great show of unconcern, but nevertheless he had something on his mind. The way he kept massaging his flaps of ears revealed his nervousness. Every now and again he lifted one booted foot and made a spur wheel spin around with the toe of the other boot.

Sharing the barn with him was his piebald horse, an animal almost as restless as himself. The barn which he was using was on ground which had belonged to a homesteader, but the main building belonging to the family had been burned down the summer before, and since then the land had been abandoned.

Not many people came that way, and

yet Murdo was on edge. He knew that all the time he rested, men acting under the orders of Long John Carrick were searching for him, and that he would have no rest at all now that Carrick was loose again, until he and his old partner, Sandy East, led the renegades to the place where their loot was buried over the border.

Red was no pessimist, but he figured that only death could get the Carrick hounds off their backs, and he did not want to die. Although he had been on the move for four years, he had not yet reached the age of his majority.

At the present moment, Red was completely alone. He had moved his whereabouts continuously for over three weeks, but now he had to consider staying in one spot, or making some sort of special move to give Sandy a chance to find him and help out. Sandy was the only person Red felt he could trust. Red was orphaned and without the benefit of any known kin. Because of this, he was difficult to get along with. He did not make friends easily, and the friends he had he worked to keep.

It galled him to draw Sandy back from his home in the next territory to help him, and yet he could scarcely help taking the course which he had done. For, after all, Sandy was tied in with him in the matter of the loot. The buried hoard was bringing them together again. Even though there was untold peril ahead for them, Red warmed at the thought of the reunion with his old partner and friend.

★　★　★

On the afternoon of the following day, Red Murdo sat his piebald pony on a hillock about a furlong south of a small but growing community known as Little Canyon. This settlement was three miles south-west of Cochise Creek and had come into being because certain types of travellers preferred to use the rather steep defile through the canyon as a short cut between the towns to eastward and westward.

The normal route was to ride into the county seat, Cochise Creek, and then come out again. This was a straightforward enough journey, but it took upwards of two hours longer than the short cut through the canyon.

The county seat was a little too 'hot' for a once-wanted small-time renegade such as the Kid. Moreover, he would not be able to pull the sort of stunt he had in mind if he used the bigger place. Besides, the wrong bunch of people might be waiting there, and then he would be grabbed before Sandy had the time to show up and find him.

One thing Red hoped for most fervently. He hoped that Long John's minions would not get their hands upon him before Sandy East had shown up. So the time had come to make his 'play'. He was about to make an open, foolish move, which should bring Sandy hurrying to his base, provided that nothing went wrong.

And Red hoped against hope that nothing would go wrong. In the past, he had taken risks. Often they had led to no profit, and other times they had brought him trouble. Sometimes from the law, and sometimes from other outlaws. He licked his lips as he contemplated action. Sandy had had the time to read the message and get into the county. It was time to make the move which would bring him into final contact.

* * *

As Red walked the piebald into the main street of Little Canyon, Hick Gorden, the keeper of the big mercantile at the west end, came through from the rear of the building and opened up the street door, which had been locked during the usual time of siesta.

Hick glanced up and down the street, as he always did at opening time, but nothing he saw occasioned any special interest. The store-keeper was fifty-six years of age, a paunchy man with a bald head, a green eye shield and big flat feet in strong leather boots. He was assisted in the running of the store by his wife, an even fatter person, but she never showed herself after midday until early in the evening. She was at that time snoring on the double bed, upstairs.

No less than six men, four white Americans and two Mexicans, were sleeping on benches up against the fronts of the buildings under the sidewalk awnings. None of them so much as moved as the piebald pony plodded past them. Red went about five yards beyond the mercantile before tethering it to the rail.

For upwards of two minutes, he had been on tenterhooks in case anyone who shouldn't happened to see his face. He had no mask across it up to that time, but his features had been concealed by a pocket handkerchief so that he could not be surprised into giving away his identity.

He stepped to the street door of the

mercantile, peered into it to accustom his eyes to the gloom, and casually pulled his blue bandanna across the lower half of his face. He murmured: 'Here we go again, Sandy, old buddy,' and stepped indoors.

The tinkling bell rang, startling the owner, who would have gambled that no one would come to buy anything for over half an hour. Hick Gorden appeared through a curtain at the rear, leaned his head back to peer at him from under his eye shield, and suddenly gaped when he saw the mask and the revolver which was pointed at him.

Red motioned for him to come out into the centre of the floor. Hick kept silent and did what was suggested without protest, although his nerves made him almost fall over some casks of vegetables and other comestibles. Red pulled down two or three leather belts, hung up for sale, and used them to truss the poor man's ankles and wrists.

Hick looked uncomfortable, all bent

up on the counter, but he still did not make any sound, and the chance was taken away from him by a gag made out of one of his most costly bandannas. Red sighed, holstered his gun, and started to fill a small sack with coins and notes from first one cash till and then the other.

As an afterthought he snatched up a bag of Bull Durham tobacco and a packet of papers. Hick followed his movements, saw him looking for matches and indicated where they were with a sidelong glance of his eyes. Red fitted a few into the band of his hat, patted his victim gently on the thigh, and withdrew, using the front entrance again.

The same men were still sleeping. Red waited until he was in the saddle, then he threw a stone which he had picked up earlier at the nearest of the sleepers. He scored a hit which roused the fellow. While the disturbed man was looking round, Red let out a blood-curdling yell which disturbed the others. After that, he used his spurs and went down the street as fast as his cayuse would carry him. When the town marshal's office was twenty yards away, Red slowed, knocking up dust. He turned the mount's head towards the office, hefted the heavy loot bag in his hand and tossed it skilfully towards the window.

The glass pane was hit squarely. The bag went through, and glass and shards were strewn in all directions. Red used the spurs again. He was still youthful enough to get some small joy out of the consternation he would leave in his wake, but he had no intention of being caught.

He waited until the startled marshal and his deputy had emerged on to the sidewalk and raced back indoors to get their weapons, then he turned abruptly into a side turning and headed north. This street was even quieter than the first.

Presently, as the uproar on Main developed, he pulled his bandanna back into the proper place, slumped in the saddle as though he had ridden a long way, and turned once again, this time to go in a westerly direction.

Still well ahead of those who sought him, he worked his way clear of the town's boundary and followed an ill-marked old animal track towards the north-west. He had pulled his stunt. The publicity would follow, and, with luck, Sandy East would hear about it, come rushing to the spot, and remember certain things which had worked for them in the past. If he did, they would meet. And things would be different.

*   *   *

Early that same evening, three riders covered in trail dust came down the track which led from Cochise Creek towards Little Canyon. They were irritable through the heat and a long way past the beer which they had taken on in the county seat.

Russ Blankers, their leader, was a big full-figured man in his middle forties with the small, dark, cunning eyes of a bear, and a fleshy mouth which his gingery beard did little to conceal. An insect or two had hidden in the beard and this made him grub around with long horny finger nails to try and remove the unwanted visitors.

Blankers was a little under six feet tall, but his bulk made him seem bigger. His fourteen stones hung heavily on the broad back of a powerful roan which had carried him for the past three months. Failing in his search, he turned his efforts elsewhere, flapping the leather vest which hung over his sweat-stained grey shirt. Next, he lifted his big grey stetson to scratch his head. He dented it again at the front before replacing it.

The man riding a white stallion on the left side of him remarked: 'I think we ain't goin' to get no place. It's a year or two since the Coyote Kids worked together, an' they must have learned a thing or two to keep out of trouble. So I don't reckon we're goin' to find them, whatever the Boss says.'

As though to add weight to his statement, 'Doc' Small snapped a match stick between his teeth. He was eight years younger than Blankers, and quite different in build. His features were thin, his face pale. The eyes betrayed his restlessness. They smouldered at times. Small was no doctor, but if he had had a black bag to go with his jacket of the same colour, he might have passed for a medical man. His undented hat and fawn buttoned vest showed a certain style, a touch of class.

Style was a thing which Ned Holder, the third member of the party, lacked. He was the youngest of the trio, a beefy man with a red face, an abundance of freckles and a broken Roman nose which seemed more ugly on account of the wide, thin, turned-down mouth underneath it.

Holder's high-pitched snigger served as an answer of sorts to Small's observation. He adjusted the slant of his narrow-brimmed stetson and brushed his punch-thickened ears more closely to the sides of his head.

'All the same, we'll have to keep a-looking' like Long John ordered,' he remarked.

Small and Holder glanced across at Blankers for his comment, but he remained silent for another five minutes. In fact, until a family wagon started to come up the trail from Little Canyon in the opposite direction.

As riders and wagon came together, Blankers showed his best trail-side manner, doffing his hat to an elderly woman and beaming at the veteran on the box as though he had come all the way to Little Canyon just to pass the time of day with him.

After the obvious pleasantries had been exchanged, Blankers raised his sketchy brows and asked: 'Anything very excitin' been happenin' in Little Canyon lately? Anything to write home about?'

The woman smiled thinly, shrugging the shawl more closely round her shoulders, waiting for her husband to open up.

'There was a ruckus of sorts, a few hours ago. Some darned young fool moseyed into the mercantile store, tied up the owner an' filled a bag with money. Only he couldn't have meant real trouble because he flung the bag of loot clean through the window of the marshal's office as he was a-ridin' down the street! After that, everybody lost track of him. Couldn't say which direction he took. But the town marshal sure is angry about his window comin' in when he was sleepin', an' the storekeeper is quietly puttin' it around that the deputy an' the jailor picked up a few dollars for themselves when they collected up the loot from the office floor.'

The old fellow went off into a paroxysm of silent laughter, which Russ Blankers seemed too polite to interrupt. He addressed his next question to the woman.

'Tell me, ma'am, did the marshal

have any idea as to the identity of the young galoot who caused the trouble?'

'Are you askin' if he knew who he was? Men up an' down the street was sayin' the whole thing smacked of the Coyote Kids, but they ain't been around lately. So maybe it was jest some other kid doin' it for a prank. Anyways, we don't rightly know. We're strangers in these parts.'

Blankers conscientiously went through the polite motions of a farewell greeting, but really he was as excited as his two henchmen. As soon as the wagon had rolled beyond them, Holder and Blankers turned on Small, who was looking a little aggrieved.

'So we ain't likely to find the Coyote Kids, huh? Well, Doc, I beg to differ. In fact, if our luck's in, I'd say we'll be usin' the same building as one of them before the sun goes down!'

Holder thought of all kinds of things to say, but instead of talking he sniggered again. Blankers thought for a minute or two, then he led them off the track on the west side.

He was muttering into his beard as the other two riders came close up on either side. 'The Kids, they had this plan. One of them would pull a stunt which the other would recognise. After that, it was always a matter of lookin' in the same direction, the north-west, if I remember rightly. One, two or three miles from town.'

Blankers sniggered for a change and this surprised the other two.

'I was thinkin' that with a bit of luck we might get both the Coyote Kids at the same time!'

7

Russ Blankers screwed the muzzle of a six-gun into the ear of Red Murdo about an hour before midnight. Red had watched out for his friend for three hours or more, and then drowsiness had overtaken him and he had gone to sleep on the wooden table of the unused sod dug-out which he had chosen for the rendezvous spot.

Red was awake in a flash, and squinting up to see if Sandy was playing a trick on him.

'If that's you, Sandy, boy, I sure don't think that's funny,' he grumbled.

Blankers laughed out loud, but he kept the gun in the same place and did not take his eyes off his victim. Small and Holder eyed him over with frank curiosity and wondered if he had changed, and by how much. Red's face blanched. He knew now that what he had most feared had happened.

Long John's oldest and most sea-soned hands had grabbed him before Sandy found the rendezvous spot. He was in real trouble. Blinking rapidly, but otherwise keeping very still, Red asked: 'What can I do for you, boys?'

No one answered. The intruders were enjoying the situation.

'That *is* you, ain't it, Russ, an' you have Ned and Doc with you? Why all this funny stuff with the gun muzzle in my ear? We've ridden before, but you never greeted me in this way before. Did I upset something you were settin' up for yourself? If I did, I can assure you it was an accident. Ain't no cause to take offence over it, either. Will you kindly take that gun out of my ear?'

Holder lit a candle and Blankers obliged. Small moved around, collect-ing up the obvious weapons and checking over Red's person for others. When it was clear that he was harmless, the three of them backed off, and

Holder voiced the first query.

'Say, Red, have you seen that buddy of yours lately? What was his name? Sandy? Sandy East?'

Red supported himself on an elbow when the immediate menace receded. He appeared to withdraw into himself when the question was asked about his friend. He was thinking that this present menace was as great a danger to Sandy as it was to himself. He was determined to say nothing. Not even to tell lies. That could come later, when Blankers got playful, as he was bound to do.

Blankers said: 'Save your breath, Ned, Sandy ain't here. Red was waitin' for him. So we'll do the same, eh? How about some sleep? How about you keepin' the first night watch, Doc?'

The tall lean figure of Small tensed up, but he nodded in agreement, and within ten minutes he was the only man awake in the sod hut.

★ ★ ★

Small turned over his watch to Holder, and he in turn passed it to Blankers. The Doc was back on duty when the dawn broke, and still there was no sign of Sandy East. The thin man had filled the dug-out with tobacco smoke by a half hour after dawn and that had the effect of making the others cough and start the day.

Holder did the cooking for breakfast, out of doors. Small and Blankers took it in turn to keep watch, though the quality of the watching was not so keen. Red was given a few bacon rashers to keep him happy, and to soften him up for what was to come.

The prisoner liked bacon, and he had few illusions about what was to follow. If this was to be his last meal, then he would enjoy it. As the coffee came to an end, Blankers gave the first intimation as to what lay ahead.

'Red, in a little while we're goin' to take a ride, all four of us. Oh, we'll keep a lookout for Sandy, don't bother your head about that. We want you to know that a whole lot depends upon your attitude towards us when we make the next stop. We'll have questions to ask, an' we need answers. Long John is the man who's really askin'.'

'I'll see what I can do when the time comes,' Red replied.

His voice was firm enough, but his inner misgivings were not far below the surface.

* * *

An hour later, Blankers called a halt. The other three reined in at once. All of them surveyed the immediate terrain, having an idea what was to take place. This new location was about two miles north-west of Little Canyon.

Blankers had halted them on the rim of a natural hollow with scrub pine fringing it to the north and east. About fifty yards to westward a large sprawling outcrop of once molten rock made a jagged gash above the long grass and fern-grown earth.

Directly north of the hollow was a long, widening valley between two hills which petered out into level ground not very far apart. Perhaps the terrain had the deepest effect upon Murdo, who had no false illusions about the invidiousness of his position.

Blankers dismounted casually enough. The others did the same, and Holder moved the horses round the rim of the hollow, into the trees on the east side. Small and Blankers walked down into the centre of the hollow with Murdo between them.

'How good is your memory, Red?' Blankers enquired, while they were still walking.

'On some things it's all right. On others not so good,' Red replied guardedly.

'Think about that loot you came across with your pardner, Sandy, the time when some of the boys were after you to settle a few differences between us.'

'I remember how it was found, all

right, but where it went to is another matter.'

'You mean you can't remember where it was buried?'

'That's about the size of things, Russ. If my memory had been good on that score, as like as not I'd have had it out before this an' become rich.'

He forced a grin, but it was not a success. Small and Blankers exchanged glances. Blankers called out an instruction to Holder, who came to join them, carrying with him a branding iron which belonged to the bearded man.

'I never did hear the story of this brand, Russ,' Holder remarked, as he handed it over.

Blankers held it up. While he studied it with the sky showing through the device at the end, Small put together the makings of a fire and coaxed it into flame. Red shuddered. He quaked inwardly. Now, he no longer wanted his friend with him. The opposition was too deadly.

'It's no brand in particular, Ned. Jest

a reminder of the days when I was an honest man, when I used my strength for the benefit of a rich rancher. One of my specialities was the branding iron. I was adept at catchin' a cow, throwin' it and brandin' it. I used to like to smell the singeing of the hide, and occasionally the smell burnin' horn gives off. Did you ever have that sort of experience, Red?'

The prisoner swallowed hard, and shook his head. 'I'll believe all you say about your skills with the iron, but if you're figurin' on pullin' some sort of trick with it, it won't work, Russ. Ask your questions, an' I'll give you what answers I can, an' let that be an end to it.'

No sort of change showed in the cunning eyes of the bearded man. He nodded, as though agreeing with what Red said, but at the same time he advanced to the fire and thrust the iron into it. Holder and Small grabbed Murdo as though they had done this routine several times before. They trussed his hands and feet again and pushed him down on the grass not far from the fire.

'I want you to sit real still while I give you a demonstration of my skill, Red,' Blankers murmured. 'A still audience is the best kind, I always think. So don't go gettin' worked up over anything. It'll all work itself out in a short time.'

Blankers' sidekicks hovered about and smoked rather furiously while the iron heated up. Red knew the signs all too well. He was about to be threatened with the iron. Blankers babbled on about it, saying that the cross within a circle was a brand made up by himself, in a smithy while the smith was out slaking his thirst.

'Now watch, Red. See how it works. This is good for your education!'

First, Blankers applied the hot iron to the bark of a fallen tree. The usual sizzling was followed by a small, smelly column of smoke. After that, the bearded man looked around for more material on which to demonstrate. In his back pocket he found an old square of leather. He was staring hard at it when Doc Small distracted him.

'Russ, I believe I'll go an' give my stallion a groomin'. If I find any more leather or anything up there, I'll let you know.'

Blankers glowered at him, and shrugged indifferently. The iron was just out of the fire again when Ned Holder also hurried away from the bottom of the hollow. He called over his shoulder that he, too, wanted to groom his horse, and that left only the tormentor and the tormented.

The cropping horses had gone down the slope on the east side, so that they were out of sight from the hollow. Murdo found himself peering after the retreating figures with a great longing for them to stay welling up inside of him. Not that their presence would disturb Blankers' performance. He was too determined, too vicious to be put off by underlings.

Blankers saw Murdo as the source of

infinitely valuable information, and he was determined, if possible, to have it before he reported to Long John Carrick, who was due in the county seat at any time.

The bearded man went close to the prisoner with an innocent smile on his face. He showed the square of leather as a conjurer might before performing a trick. Then he held it in the air, and dropped it on the hot brand. The leather sizzled a little, but bounced off and fell to the ground.

'Not a very good trick, after all,' Blankers murmured to himself.

By way of a change, he placed the leather on the fallen tree, and jabbed at it like a swordsman might do. At the second attempt, he connected with it and held the pose. The hot brand burned into the leather until the cross and circle symbol had gone all the way through.

Blankers straightened up, quite pleased with his effort. He collected the smoking leather and tossed it across to his victim. Heat and smoke briefly affected Red as the leather dropped on his shirt and then fell away beside him.

The tormentor put the iron back in the fire, and relaxed, mopping his brow with a dark bandanna. All the time he worked, his eyes were on Red, who writhed on the floor, to no avail. The short pieces of whipcord were biting into his wrists and ankles as he struggled, but his bonds held.

'Where was it you said the loot was buried, lad?' Blankers asked.

'I didn't say, an' I can't remember,' Red replied hoarsely. 'I wasn't fit at the time. I had a fever or something. A short time in my life is blank. So why don't you quit this — this act an' try something else? I tell you I don't know!'

Blankers made a round 'O' of his fleshy mouth. He blew into the fire, and casually extracted the branding iron once again. The heat of it made him hold it away from him. He muttered something about the action of great heat on human flesh and began to approach his victim.

Red was dripping perspiration. He saw the hot emblem coming nearer to his face, and the hard cruel countenance held back behind it. Small and Holder were out of sight. They were not even watching from a distance. If there was to be any sort of diversion, Red would have to make it himself. Even if he survived, he did not want to face the world with scars on his countenance. In the last few seconds, a shaky off-the-cuff sort of plan began to evolve in his mind. Blankers was not seeing him perfectly because of the shimmer of heat between them. The bearded man was moving closer and beginning to crouch, as Red withdrew his head and shoulders as far as possible.

The victim bent his legs as far as they would go, and prepared to use them to his advantage. To bring down, or forcibly halt the big man, he would have to use both feet, but that was not difficult when they were secured together.

The brand was less than a foot away when Red squirmed and aimed his kick. He took an awful chance of being badly branded as he thrust up his booted feet and kicked his oppressor in the solar plexus. All the force which he could muster went into the kick. It was most effective.

Blankers dropped the iron and doubled over in pain, and through being winded, he staggered back, tripped over a branch of the fallen log, and hit the back of his head and neck against the bole. The blow he received was a sickening one, due to his excessive weight. For a time, he was stunned and unaware of what was going on around him.

Red, on the other hand, lived a long time in every fleeting second. He rolled on the ground, managed to pick up the branding iron, and coaxed the burning end towards the thong which lashed his feet together. The cord started to sizzle. He put some strain upon it, and had the satisfaction of seeing it part. Next, he started to work on his wrists, but a movement on the part of Blankers threw him in a fresh panic.

Instead, he started to run away from the spot with iron in his hand. This was the limit of his planning. He ran towards the north-west, heading for the extremity of the rocky outcrop to westward.

Blankers yelled: 'Hey, Small, Holder! The prisoner is getting away! Will you show yourselves?'

A sketchily aimed bullet flew after the fugitive, who retaliated by hurling the branding iron in the direction of Blankers. As soon as he had done it, it occurred to him that he had parted with his only weapon. Where he was running to, he did not know, but he still had strength in his limbs, and life was suddenly very precious.

Behind him, in the hollow, there were more shouts. Three six guns blazed away in his direction as he cleared the rim of the hollow in a staggering crouch and headed for the heap of upthrust rock.

8

News of Red Murdo's indiscretion had reached the county seat within a few hours, by virtue of the telegraph system. Sandy East, who arrived in town about the same time as the gossip began to go around, immediately understood what was happening, even though the actual incident was garbled and out of all proportion.

He moved to the edge of town, where he was least likely to be recognised, and saw to the needs of his horse and of himself. Then, when most people were relaxing for the evening, or going to their beds, he left the county seat again, and headed in the direction which Red would expect him.

Since dawn, on the following morning, Sandy had been very active, but he had failed to find any sort of human habitation where Red was likely to be.

At the very time when his old partner needed him most, he was sitting his buckskin with a leg crooked round the saddle horn surveying the surrounding landscape from a high point at the southern end of one of the hills above the hollow where the trouble was.

His vantage point was on the hill further westward. After mopping salt perspiration from his brow, Sandy put the glass to his eye again in the hope of seeing something significant which he had missed the first time.

The emergence of his friend was not at first noticed, because the glass was pointed further east, towards the scattering of trees below which the four horses were located. It was the first six-gun bullet which alerted Sandy; that, and a sudden glimpse of Red running hatless around the end of the outcrop.

Although in riding boots, Red was running well. He had parted with the branding iron, the significance of which would have escaped Sandy, and ducked as other bullets flew towards him. The watcher took his eyes off his friend for a few seconds, as the first of the pursuers appeared over the rim of the hollow. It was Blankers, and the view through the glass at once confirmed his identity.

Sandy was quite disturbed, having found his friend, only to know that he was in grave danger. Young East was biting his underlip and wondering how big the opposition was likely to be when he turned his attention once again to the fugitive. He was just in time to see what happened.

Within twenty yards of the end of the outcrop a fissure developed in the earth. The crack widened and twisted away towards the north-west with a scattering of rim rock on either side masking its presence. Red, who was heading straight towards it, no doubt seeking the shelter of the rocks, suddenly saw the earth gape in front of him.

He was too late to stop. Before Sandy could shout any kind of warning, Red failed to check his forward progress. With arms outstretched, and calling out briefly in despair, he plummeted into the widening crevasse with only a few small stones and an eddying of dust to mark his passage.

Sandy, rendered dry-throated with shock, squared himself up in the saddle and started to descend the tricky unbroken slope directly towards the gully. This far, the three outlaws had not noticed him. They did, however, witness Murdo's sudden disappearance, and as they were no more aware of the crevasse than he had been, they slowed up, and eyed each other for a few seconds before carrying on.

Warily, and with guns to hand, they approached the scattering of rocks which masked the gully. On the slope to northward, Sandy checked the buckskin behind a big sprawl of rock, and dismounted. He hauled his Henry rifle out of the scabbard and began to go further on foot, taking care to keep himself out of sight.

From time to time, he caught glimpses of Blankers, Small and Holder as they manoeuvred themselves among the rocks and began to look down into the depths of the crevasse. The fact that Red was down there in no way diminished their interest in him. And that meant that Sandy would have to use his weapons to distract them.

He worked his way sufficiently far down the slope to put himself in reasonable distance for rifle work, and then came to a halt. He was desperately anxious about Red's fall. Could the others, he wondered, see sufficiently well to know whether he had survived or not?

He waited and watched. Small slipped away again and returned with two lariats. That development seemed promising. They were about to descend, and that meant that Red was probably alive. They would scarcely attempt to go down into the fissure otherwise.

It was time to take a hand in the uneven performance. While Holder knotted the two lariats together, Sandy lined up his Henry on a rock between Small and Blankers. He squeezed and fired. The bullet whined through the air, hit the rock and sent dust and splinters into the faces of the two startled outlaws, who promptly ducked out of sight.

'Hell an' tarnation, that's all we need!' Blankers protested hoarsely. 'Somebody tryin' to keep us out of the gully! Why, that tricky little cuss down there might be dead if we're delayed long. What are we goin' to do about it?'

Holder suggested: 'Somebody ought to go back an' collect the rifles, otherwise that hombre could keep us pinned down for a long time!'

'You've said it, Ned,' Small put in warmly.

Blankers aimed a .44 at the source of the rifle fire. He pulled the trigger twice. As soon as this was over, he called to Holder.

'Slip away, Ned, an' get back with the guns as soon as you can! We can't all chance that rifle, the jasper knows how to fire it! So hurry it up, *muy pronto*!'

Holder dropped the lariats, quietly cursing to himself over having to take on the risky job. He moved out, but very slowly, and Sandy's probing weapon gave him several close scares. By the time he returned, Blankers and Small had guessed the identity of the gunman holding them off, although they had seen nothing to confirm their guesswork.

Five minutes elapsed after Holder's return. When he had recovered his breath, and his partners had fired off a few angry rounds to restore themselves to normality, he enquired: 'How are we goin' to get rid of that hombre an' get down to Murdo?'

'We worked it out while you were away, Ned,' Small called to him. 'Murdo will have to wait. You an' me, we slip away round the east side of that fellow's position, while Russ, here, goes round the other side. Do you get the plan?'

'Sure, who goes first, an' who covers who?' Holder queried.

'We go first. I'll lead the way, so make good use of that weapon of yours so I can make it to the nearest rock east of the gully. Savvy?'

Blankers and Holder did the necessary shooting to keep Sandy's head down while the initial move was made. All three were used to this kind of manoeuvre and they did their job well. At a time when Sandy was thinking that he would have to conserve his ammunition, they started to spread out and surround his position.

The swale which separated the two rolling hills was modest in width. Every few yards there were rocks across it, rocks which perhaps had arrived there when the hills were higher and the swale was deeper. However, they had arrived, they were of great interest and utility to Small and Holder as they started to encroach upon Sandy East's position.

★ ★ ★

Sandy's anxiety began to give way to pessimism. Red was down a hole, and almost certainly injured. And he was pinned down on a rocky hill slope by three determined killers. No wonder the mature Long John gangs had always regarded the Coyote Kids as small fry.

For a time, he was content to put down an occasional shot as Small or Holder made a move. Blankers dropped out of the reckoning for a while. He was taking his time about rounding the end of the fissure prior to moving up the west side of Sandy's position.

The young man thought about the whole situation. This location was sufficiently far off the beaten track for this trio to keep after him all day. Not that he could hold them off all that time, not without help. It looked as if this day had put the Coyote Kids firmly into the clutches of Long John Carrick.

Poor Red didn't even remember the exact location of the buried loot, due to his ill health at the time. Maybe Blankers and his boys would leave Red down below, when they found out who was shooting at them. The onus would then be upon Sandy to tell them what their Boss so badly wanted to know.

He found himself hoping against hope that Billy Bartram was still rooting for him, and within striking distance.

* * *

In actual fact, Billy had made excellent time since he detoured to Junction and came on westward. He had arrived in the county seat within hours of Sandy's arrival, and at once started to contact his superior and one or two other men who had a special interest in the Long John Carrick business.

Within the hour, permission was given for Billy to follow up the lead which might take him to the notorious Long John, or, more to the point, Long John's minions who were active before the gang boss arrived to take over control.

Through the telegraph, the county authorities were soon wised up to the small but spectacular happening in Little Canyon. Obviously, Sandy was being drawn by his friend to the vicinity of that small town. Billy, therefore, left the county seat at dawn and rode south in the general direction of the settlement.

Because the dun had covered a lot of ground previously, and also because it might be required to use its stamina a whole lot more in the near future, Billy was content for it merely to stroll along the trail. He rested it and watered it, and so, purely by good luck, he was in a position close enough to be on hand when the shooting started.

As the first shots echoed across from the west, he glanced up at a natural slope on the west side of the trail and wondered what the odds were against one of the Coyote Kids being involved in the fracas. It occurred to him that he was acting quite foolishly when he sent the dun off-trail to westward to investigate.

The echoes of rifle fire carried well. There were pauses between significant exchanges. This was no one out on a hunting expedition, unless the quarry was human. He knew that if he kept moving in the same direction that sooner later he would come upon men intent upon a blood-letting.

Unevenness in the terrain, and his own anxiety to reach the scene of the exchanges quickly, brought him out on to the slopes of the hill to north-eastward of the hollow where Murdo had been held. But the action had passed from the hollow and from Murdo before he reached the area. Now, three guns were pinning down a single rifle on the slopes of the hill opposite.

As soon as he came around a spur of the hill, Billy reined in and took stock of the scene through his glass. There was still nothing at all visible to show him that he had stumbled upon anything to do with the Coyote Kids. For upwards of two minutes he panned the glass before one of the attackers darted from one rock to another five yards away.

No sooner had the fellow moved than the single rifle on the hillside put a shell his way, and a second man, not at this time going forward, aimed at the place from which the shot had come. A minute later, another man, hidden well over to westward of the hill under fire, started to put in bullets from another angle. Three bullets, fired with a short interval between each, had the lone man edging about behind his rock cover. He was certainly beginning to feel the squeeze.

The two attackers on the valley floor saw a signal which was hidden from Sandy and Billy. They kept low, while Blankers tried the effect of his voice.

'Hey, you up there! We take it you're a friend of Red Murdo! Is that correct?'

No answer from the hillside, but Billy

on his hill had heard the shouted query and he was grinning eagerly, because he felt sure that the man he was about to defend was Sandy East. Without haste, Billy dismounted and hauled his Winchester out of the scabbard.

'If you are Sandy East you can prevent all this shooting! All you have to do is come down here an' give us certain information! We couldn't help what happened to Red, he ran and fell down a gully, as you may have seen!'

This second attempt to cut short the conflict failed. Sandy's spirits were low, but he had used the lull to reload, and now he aimed his Henry in the direction of the voice and cut short a third appeal by sending a bullet far too close for comfort.

Billy found himself a useful vantage point behind two rocks. They protected him, and yet did not altogether hide him from the men he intended to shoot at. The names of the attackers were not known to him, but he felt justified in firing without warning, and in shooting to kill.

The firing from the valley floor started all over again. The tension was back. Billy had his Winchester aimed at a spot half-way between the rocks which sheltered the two attackers. There was a brief pause, and then Ned Holder boldly rolled sideways and started on a jinxing run which would take him to another rock some ten yards away.

He had gone all of three yards when Billy's weapon belched flame for the first time. Holder paused in midstride as the bullet hit him high in the chest. He staggered and recovered, but a second bullet from the same gun hit him lower down and brought him crashing down to the earth, where he lost his hat and his gun, and shortly afterwards, his life.

Small was considerably shaken by this sudden development. Their little scheme was starting to go sour on them. In a sudden flurry of activity, he moved his position to give more protection from the hill to the east, but a change of strategy on the part of the latest comer negatived his effort.

Billy was aiming for ricochets. His second shot nicked Small's left arm. The third was the lethal one. It came off rock at an oblique angle, entered his body at the throat and travelled to his brain, where it stopped. His rifle was accidentally discharged. It fell, so that it showed beyond the screening stones and Billy felt reasonably sure that he had scored another kill.

Russ Blankers' weapon remained ominously quiet. Sandy East was the first to break the silence.

He called out hoarsely: 'Billy? Is that you?'

'Sure, I'm with you amigo! An' the menace has faded on this side! Keep an eye open for that other fellow, though! He may be closer than you think!'

Sandy replied suitably, and the waiting game was resumed. Billy had worked a surprise once, and Blankers, bereft of his henchmen as far as he knew, was not going to be caught between the fire of two men. Consequently, he started to pull out, and to make his way by the safest route possible towards the waiting horses below the hollow.

9

The fighting with guns had passed its high point. Billy left the onus for what happened next to Sandy, and Sandy wanted to pull out. Uppermost in his mind was the need to get close to Red Murdo and find out exactly what had happened to him.

With this in mind, Sandy fired one or two probing shots in the direction of the spot where Blankers had been holed up. There was no answering fire. They waited, and then, just occasionally, they heard small sounds which suggested the top renegade was pulling out. He worked his way down off the slope and back round the fissure until he was in a position to cross the hollow and get to his mount.

Billy, who became aware of the movements towards the end, sent a rifle bullet at extreme range to help Blankers on his way. The latter rounded up the horses and struck out towards the east. Billy then stood up and called out again.

Ten minutes later, the allies came together, shook hands, and walked down towards the gully where Red had disappeared. They had their mounts with them, but the horses were cast loose until it became clear that one or both would be needed to lift Red out of the ground.

Billy knotted lariats, but Sandy insisted on going below himself while Billy stood guard. The upper end of the two lariats was attached to the saddle horn of the dun, which took the strain as Sandy climbed lower and generally made the descent easier.

Sandy indicated briefly that he had arrived, but called up no information for a while.

Billy waited, and wondered. 'Sandy, is there anything you can tell me?'

The younger man made a sound which could have been described as choking. At length, he had his voice under control. 'He's jest died, Billy. All he could manage was a smile, an' that was a brief one. I figure he was all broken up inside with the fall. What are we goin' to do with him now?'

'As he has no folks, we could bury him some place close, out in the open, but I don't advise that. Why not let me take him into Cochise Creek? I think I have enough influence there to have him nicely buried at Boot Hill! Besides, Long John will have to know the worst. We could hang around for a day or so, an' see what happens after that.'

Sandy did not appear to be too happy about Billy's advice, but he gave his assent to the suggestion, and presently they were co-operating to have the dead body removed. The lariats went down again, and soon a very chastened Sandy was back on level ground.

'Some friend I turned out to be, turnin' up when I did — too late!'

'Don't blame yourself, Sandy. You

couldn't help the way things turned out. At least Red got a glimpse of you before he died. Your presence gave him some satisfaction, an' that's for sure. Ride a little way with me towards the county seat, and then cut out some place till we see how the opposition is massin' after this setback. I'll see to the burial, an' you'll be around.'

Sandy nodded. He personally saw to Red being draped over Billy's horse before mounting up on his own. Unfortunately, Blankers had taken Red's horse with him. No doubt he had done it on purpose so as to prevent his enemies from getting away easily. Slowly, the grim-faced pair headed towards the trail for the county seat.

* * *

Any worthwhile renegade outfit needed several calling places and a few hideouts. The one which Long John Carrick decided to use when he first arrived back in the area of the county seat was located in a hollow near a secondary creek, west of Cochise Creek. No less than two dugouts were carved out of the rear side of the hollow. About fifty yards separated them.

Russ Blankers, still leading the spare horses, appeared on the south side of the creek opposite the hideouts, and proceeded to send the horses through the ford. Three or four outlaws emerged from the dugout further east and showed a lively interest in the empty saddles, but they refrained from shouting out for further information, which they would normally have done, and instead indicated that the other dugout was occupied.

Blankers guessed at the arrival of Long John, and he reflected that the morning's setbacks could not have come at a worst time. The bearded man shooed the spare horses aside, walked his own up to the dugout, and there dismounted rather heavily.

'That you, Russ?' Long John enquired.

'Sure, it's me, Boss. Glad to have you

back with us. I had hoped to bring you good news right off, but I've got to admit a setback. Things didn't turn out as I had planned. Not at all, they didn't.'

Long John was stretched out on a bunk at the far side of the long earth-walled room. He was two inches over six feet tall, and his boots stuck out beyond the end. He was a big-boned man with heavy shoulders. His complexion was a rich one, compounded of sunburn and a certain redness connected with high living and blood pressure. He had a long nose and small, dark, ill-assorted eyes, the whites of which were red-veined. His hair was thick, sleek and black. He wore it parted high and brushed down to the sides and back of his head. A few grey hairs were now showing in the neatly tapered sideburns. His soiled white shirt was topped with a grey cutaway coat which had seen better days. A black, low-crowned, wide-brimmed, Quaker-style hat was pushed to the back of his head.

As he turned and rested his weight on his elbow, moving a small cheroot around his fleshy lips, Blankers was thinking that he looked his forty years.

'Is it a tale of empty saddles, Russ, because I don't like that sort of thing. What sort of a home-coming does it make? Out with it!'

Blankers explained how they had acted on a hunch, and as a result they had found and jumped Murdo. His narrative slowed as the painful part came up where Red fought back and got away, and the very end of the recital, when Russ had to admit that a second intruder had killed Holder and Small, was only extracted from him with much prompting.

'An' you are sure that Red didn't know details of where the loot was buried? That he was ill or something at the time?'

To these questions Blankers answered firmly in the affirmative. He also reiterated that the first intruder was almost certainly Sandy East, who *did* have the information they sought.

'So where is the Kid now?' John asked patiently.

'Not far from here, Boss, mournin' over the loss of his pardner. If you like, I'll ride straight into town and keep a sharp watch on the comings and goings. How — how will that be?'

Long John flicked ash on the floor. He shook his head. 'Nope. You've done enough for this morning, amigo. I'll go into town an' take a look round. After all, I've paid my debt to society, an' no one is ever goin' to nail me for the Harvey Timms killin'. So why shouldn't I show myself? I'll spread it around that I'm a reformed character. No more bushwhackin' or dry-gulchin' for Long John. It'll be interestin' to see how they take the information.'

'I'll get you a horse, Boss,' Blankers offered.

The bearded man preceded his Boss and rapidly checked over the white stallion which had been the mount of Doc Small. He knew that Long John always fancied white horses, so his choice ought to please.

Two or three minutes went by, and the Boss was about to mount up when another rider came across the sloping ground on the north side on a smart stockingfoot sorrel. The outlaws using the other building swarmed out, surprised by this sudden and unexpected approach, but the tallest of them, Lofty Raymore, soon put them at ease.

'Boys, this here is my brother, Nils! How've you been, Nils, come on over here an' meet the boys!'

Nils was forking a horse which looked as if it could match the performance of any of theirs. He slipped to the ground, warmly shook hands with his brother, and was introduced to two other men, Jack Drex and his cousin, Miff Thorn. Drex was nearing forty, a fair, bald-headed man who sported a short beard over his lantern jaw. As he nodded to the visitor, the broken rim of his black hat flapped. Thorn was a few years younger than

Drex. He was homely-looking, with a bony forehead and a flattened nose. He had heavy hips and thighs which made him slow-moving when out of the saddle.

'How come you drop in on us like this, Nils?'

'I've been followin' a trail which led into this area, Lofty. It started way back towards Texas. I took up with a young woman, name of Della, an' we've been followin' her restless little brother for many a day now.'

Some of the interest went out of the nearest faces. Long John, who was standing about ten yards away, with his back to the group, listening, began to shoot the kind of looks at Blankers which suggested that Nils Raymore ought to have remained a stranger.

'But wait till you hear her brother's name, Lofty. Sandy. Sandy East. None other than one of the Coyote Kids! How about that? But I guess you boys are already wise to the kind of loot the Kids buried?'

Drex, Thorn and the brother nodded, but they waited for Long John to comment. His interest had suddenly brightened. He crossed over, introduced himself, and sent Lofty away to get some coffee for the newcomer.

'You said something about Sandy East's sister, Della. Is she with you?'

'Sure enough, Long John. She's occupyin' a large room at the Creek Hotel back there in town. You ought to come along and meet her some time.'

'I had it in mind to visit her right now, on my own, Nils. You understand that a man in my business has to keep a sharp eye on the kind of folks who get close to him. I'm interested in Sandy, an' the loot he knows about, too. So we're in the same business, huh?

'Now, why don't you settle down an' have a long talk with Lofty, here, while I ride into town, make certain enquiries and pay my respects to your lady friend?'

The gang leader sounded cordial enough, but it was clear from the faces of the other outlaws in the group that Nils did not have any option. He agreed with alacrity. Long John mounted up, doffed his hat at them and drew and spun his six-guns. Almost as an afterthought, he called: 'Boys, why don't you draw lots for that fine black gelding which belonged to poor Ned Holder?'

Five minutes later, after the leader had left, the gelding passed into the possession of Lofty Raymore.

★　★　★

The past few days had been frustrating ones for Della Rhodes, but she had patience, and she had never expected to become rich without working for it. As soon as Nils showed restlessness in the county seat, Della had a feeling that she would have company. She was not sure who it was likely to be, but she wanted to make a good impression.

She waited for about an hour reclining on a long couch, combing her great long bell of copper-coloured hair, and dreaming about the future. It was only when the heavy steps came up to her landing and hovered outside the door that she showed signs of her normal restless energy.

In a flash she was on her feet, tidying her lace-trimmed white blouse, smoothing down her figure-hugging grey skirt and wondering what best she could do for effect. A loud, confident knock came on the door panel. In her stockinged feet she crossed to a long mirror. There, facing her reflection, she pulled up her skirt and made out that she was adjusting her garter.

'Come in!' she called sharply.

Long John swung open the door, and stepped inside, moving quickly. His eyes went straight to the attractive figure in front of the mirror, as they should have done. He gallantly backed to the door, but closed it behind him and rested against it.

Della looked up, rather belatedly, said: 'Why, hello, Nils — oh!' She covered her face as though blushing in surprise and hurriedly lowered her skirt. Still apparently embarrassed, she crossed to the window and averted her face.

'Sir, you have me at a disadvantage. I thought you were another.'

'Ma'am, I hadn't thought to put you at a disadvantage, but you did ask me to come in, an' I do know your friend, Nils. I've seen him this morning.'

Long John removed his hat, and waited with his hand on the door knob, though he had no intention of withdrawing. Della knew who he was, and she was making the most of an interesting situation. She knew John was not long released, but his period of incarceration did not seem to have spoiled his looks.

Suddenly she smiled. Her face had assumed a bewitching look.

'I know you by what I've heard about you, Mr Carrick. Perhaps you'd care to sit on the couch an' tell me what it was you had in mind to visit me about.'

John smiled. He moved towards the furniture, but declined to sit down until Della was seated first. She squatted neatly about a yard away from him, and draped her arms round her knees. A quizzical smile started the visitor on his explanation.

'Am I to call you Miss Della?' he queried.

'Call me Della, if you care to. I'm Mrs Della Rhodes, a widow, you see. Is this something to do with my brother?'

John gestured with his hand and nodded. 'Sure. Your brother, Sandy, and I were well known to each other before I went away for my, er, long vacation. It jest so happens that Sandy an' his young friend, Red Murdo, know the location of some very valuable property.

'Now, in the past, as most folks know, I've headed one or two wild bunches and collected my pickings where I could. I want to change my ways. It has occurred to me that if I could get my hands on that property Sandy knows about, I wouldn't have to go breakin' the law any more. Do you follow me?'

'I do, indeed, John,' Della returned warmly. 'I've thought along those lines myself, ever since Sandy returned to his native territory and told me about the valuables. He mentioned a small statue of the Madonna and Child, in gold. And silver candlesticks, studded with cut diamonds, and a bag of loose diamonds, as well. A king's ransom, I would have said. But Sandy is not anxious to have anything to do with these things. I don't think he'd even show *me* where they were, an' I'm his sister. He might have to be persuaded, otherwise we'd all have to stay poor.'

John had been nodding. 'My sentiments exactly, Della. I wanted to ascertain whether you would object if it were necessary to put a little pressure on Sandy in order to bring the loot into our possession. Rest assured, if I got my hands on it I'd see the East family had a fair share!'

'I'm sure you would, John. And I'll

still keep tryin' to persuade him, of course. But the pressure business is better in your hands. You'd best know how to apply it.'

John threaded the fingers of his hands together and cracked the joints. He was feeling more confident now, and the need was not so great to show an image of gentility. Della noted the change in him. When he regarded her again, the look was a different one. He was speculating about her in a different way.

'I like the way you talk, Della, an' it's my belief your brother is in this town or near it, right now. You and I, we must keep in touch.'

He rose to his feet and moved slowly towards her. At the last moment Della stood up, looking as chic as she could manage. She tendered a hand towards him. He took it firmly and planted a kiss on the back of it. He was slow to release her, and she appeared not to want her hand back again. She moved a few inches closer to him.

Suddenly John rumbled in his throat. He pressed forward, grabbed Della in his arms and kissed her hard on the lips. As the kiss ended, she placed her hands on his chest, but the pressure was minimal. John regarded her in close-up. He was strongly-passioned and strong-willed. On this occasion his will made him let go.

As though mildly regretful of his actions, he strode to the door. Almost as an afterthought, he asked: 'May I ask what the true relationship is between yourself and Nils Raymore?'

Della nodded, swishing her hair provocatively. 'You could say he's my henchman. He's helping me towards my ambition. Jest whether he'll still be there when I achieve it, I couldn't rightly say at this moment. Adios, John.'

The renegade said his farewell and stepped out on to the landing feeling well satisfied.

10

Sheriff Tom Gore, the senior peace officer in Cochise County, Arizona territory, was a tall man in fringed buckskin with long white hair and a neatly trimmed moustache and beard. His stiff, flat-crowned, black hat added a touch of the military to his rather bizarre appearance. His single .45 Colt was low slung beside his right thigh. He stacked up to a formidable officer, and few men dared to suggest that he resembled the made-up stars of Wild West circuses.

Gore had just returned to his office around midday when Billy Bartram appeared with Red Murdo's body slung across his saddle. Red was left outside, as it was thought to be a good thing to let the news spread itself.

Indoors, Billy gave a resumé of what had happened at the shoot-out. Gore listened well, and did not interrupt until he had finished. Eventually, the senior officer fingered his beard and started to talk.

'I surely didn't think to see you back here this quickly, Billy. But things are certainly startin' to pop. So Red's dead, and Sandy is in the area. An' Long John's boys are busy, too. As like as not Long John will move around here as bold as brass in the next day or two. Tell me, what do you plan to do now?'

Billy drew easily on his smoke. 'Oh, stick around for a while. At least until after Red is buried. Then Sandy will make a move. Either he'll go back to where he came from, or he'll be pressured to go south and reveal where that old Spanish loot is buried. Me, I'm stickin' close to him to see how Carrick's boys shape up to the next challenge.

'This far three of them have been eliminated, but there were plenty of ordinary outlaws to work for Long John before he went inside. This far, none of

152

them have shown any particular interest in me. But that could all change in the near future.'

'You'll try an' let me know if you have to pull out in a hurry, Billy?'

'I'll surely do that, Tom,' Billy promised. 'My next stop is the undertaker's. An' maybe the doctor ought to take a look at Red's corpse. His fall knocked him about a lot.'

Sheriff Gore came outside and took a look for himself. He was very thoughtful when he retired into his office. No one else got to speak to him about the fatality, whereas Billy was answering brief queries all the way to the funeral parlour.

★ ★ ★

The local authorities were soon satisfied about the cause of Murdo's death. A quick burial was arranged and a ready-made coffin used. Late that same afternoon, the interment took place, and a few score people went along there, as much out of curiosity as for any other reason.

The town marshal's office was represented and Billy turned up to represent the sheriff's office. Those who were most interested in the Coyote Kids kept out of the way. By seven o'clock in the evening, the stream of visitors to Boot Hill had dwindled to nothing.

Della Rhodes then left the Creek Hotel in a dark gown and with her face veiled. She rode side-saddle on a roan mare which carried her up to the burial ground. Her interest lay in the same place as others, in fact at Red Murdo's grave. She placed a small bouquet of flowers upon it, and squatted beside it with great patience for well over an hour before she heard the first signs of another person approaching.

Sandy came across the cemetery from the west side, walking with his head held low and his hat pulled forward. Some ten yards away he paused, seemingly at a loss to know where the latest grave was to be found. He blinked as the crouched figure of his sister showed up beside it. Della was just getting up because her prolonged wait at ground level had given her a slight attack of cramp.

When she saw Sandy, she gave a sigh of relief.

'Sandy! You took your time in gettin' here to your friend's grave. Where have you been all day? And why have you been dodgin' me all the way across the territories? Are you ashamed of me, or something?'

Sandy took off his hat and smoothed out his hair, which was stuck down with perspiration. 'Nice to see you again, sis, though I can't think why you followed me here. I came along at Red's request, an' that was no sort of reason for you to follow me.'

He moved around the grave, knelt and closed his eyes, repeating soundlessly a short prayer which he had known since childhood. Della, kneeling opposite, waited impatiently for his attention. She tossed a stone against the low stone wall which was about five yards away.

At last, Sandy opened his eyes and glanced across at her. He seemed to be extremely embarrassed by her presence. His eyes said as much. He started to shake his head. Della hesitated and to avert an argument about what had been discussed before, she asked about Red's death.

'He had an accident, didn't he? Were you there when it happened?'

'Yes an' no,' Sandy murmured. 'He was bein' tortured by Long John's boys, an' then he broke away jest before I found him. In his haste to put distance between himself and the others he failed to see the ground in front of him. There was this deep gully. He fell straight into it, and the fall gave him multiple injuries. He died jest as I got to him.'

Della was thinking over these revelations with mixed feelings. It had not occurred to her that the dead youth might have been tortured for what he knew.

'He — he died almost straight away then? Maybe that was best, no time to suffer any pain.'

'If I know Red he struggled to keep alive. He was down that gully for quite a long time before I could get near him. You see there was a bout of shooting between me an' the three men who had held him prisoner.'

'An' you drove them all off?' Della queried breathlessly.

Sandy looked away. 'Not exactly, they would have taken me as well, in time, if a friend hadn't turned up to help fight them off. As it happened, two of the outlaws were killed by this friend, and the other decided to pull out. So now you know all the story.'

Sandy knew his revelations had shaken Della. But he wondered just how tough, and how determined she really was. After all, she had covered hundreds of miles presumably just to keep in touch with him on account of the buried loot which he knew about.

'Were these men who attacked you part of the Carrick gang?'

'They were, indeed, and they're very dirty fighters, especially when they want something in particular. Is there anything else you want to know? You ought to get some satisfaction after your long trip.'

This carefully worded retort brought a flash of anger to Della. She lifted up the small bouquet, fought for control again, and lowered it gently upon the mound.

'Who was this friend you spoke of, the one who saved you from the outlaws?'

'A man named Billy Bartram, a peace officer who works in this county.'

'Billy Bartram? But I know a man of that name. The son of a preacher back in New Mexico. Could it be the same man, do you think?'

'Sure it's the same man,' Sandy replied bitterly. 'You'll be able to call on his Pa again on the way back to Texas.'

Della massaged her ankles, fidgeting restlessly. She knew the answer to her next question before she asked it. 'What are you plannin' to do now, Sandy?'

'Why, go back to Texas, where I came from. What else? All I came here for was to help my buddy, Red. An' now he's dead, so I can't help any more. So there's nothing to keep me, is there?'

Sandy stood up. He toyed with his hat as he glanced back down the hill towards the nearest buildings. Della's almost silent weeping took him by surprise. He felt pangs of affection for her which he had thought were dead. Rounding the grave he knelt beside her.

'Why, what is it? There's something you haven't told me yet.'

He took the small handkerchief from her and dabbed her eyes with it. A fleeting thought cut across her mind. This little brother of hers was a darned sight more handsome than Nils Raymore, or even Long John Carrick.

'I came this way, little brother, with a man named Nils Raymore.'

'I know you did. What else?'

'Well, I think I may have made a bad mistake. I was lonely, since my husband died, and this Nils came around. I'm beginning to have my doubts about him. He's been away from me for several hours today. He has a brother in the Carrick gang. An' that ain't good. We've talked about that — that loot, recently. And Nils' attitude has changed. He says the Carrick boys could be very nasty with me if I didn't use my influence with you to have you show them where the loot is.

'Sandy, I'm frightened. You said yourself your friend was tortured by Carrick's men. I think Nils will side with the gang if they come lookin' for me. I don't know where to turn, really.'

The young man groaned. 'You're in a spot, sis, an' no mistake. How do you think I could help, other than show this unholy outfit where the loot is?'

'Well, if you wouldn't mind makin' a gesture for the time being . . . '

'What do you mean, a gesture?'

'I thought maybe you could leave this place and ride south, as though you were headin' for the spot where the loot was buried. That way, any pressure which was building up against me in this place would be lifted for a time. Maybe on another occasion I could slip away. What do you think?'

Sandy's unlined face contrived to look set and bitter as he thought over the possibilities. Unfortunately, he could think of no way in which to ensure his sister's safety. Every idea he thought of had a snag to it. Eventually, he turned to her again.

'You think if I headed towards the border for a while, things would be easier for you, sis?'

'I surely do, Sandy, it's the only way I can see out of my present predicament. Will you do it, for my sake?'

He wanted to tell her that if she had not left Texas in such a big hurry she would now be completely safe, and unknown to Long John, probably. The tearful expression on her face prevented him from chiding her. He offered no criticism.

'I'll do it, then, but make sure of this. Whatever I do is highly dangerous. An' I'll get no pleasure out of it. None at all. When I go, the folks who watch me will know I've pulled out. You, I suppose, will have to travel some little way in the same direction. I don't know how or when I'll be able to get in touch with you, so don't hold out any false hopes, eh?'

Having said his piece, he put a hand under her arm and hoisted her to her feet. He kissed her lightly on the cheek, and then on the lips, when she craved more affection.

'I'll try not to make any more calls on you, little brother, an' I'm sorry for all the trouble I've caused this far. Do we say goodbye right here?'

Sandy nodded. He patted her shoulder and went away across the little plots. 'Get back to your hotel an' try to sleep easy,' he called quietly.

And then he was gone. Della left

almost at once. About fifty yards along the wall, Sandy vaulted over. He came back along the other side until he found Billy, sitting with his back to the wall. He sat down beside him and accepted a smoke.

'Well, amigo, that was my big sister, Della, as you know. What did you make of the exchanges?'

Billy studied Sandy's face before replying. He could see that he was very sensitive on the question of his kin. Perhaps it was because Della was his only close blood relation.

'Somebody's been to work on her, Sandy. Maybe it was Raymore, like she said. As far as I could tell, she's really worried. She could also be very determined, on her own account. I wouldn't like to work out her feelings in detail, because I don't know her that well. It could be a mixture of fear and greed.'

Sandy was slow to react to these observations. At length, he said: 'She really was shaken when I told her about

Red being tortured. I wonder if she was fearful on her own account, or on mine?'

A short silence built up between the two friends. Billy gripped Sandy by the upper arm. 'Think about it some more. The main thing is, you've decided to ride a little further south. When will you be startin' out?'

'Are you goin' along with the action, Billy?'

'Certain sure, Sandy. Count me in. The deaths of three hired killers was not what I had in mind. Besides, I might come in useful again at another venue.'

'I'll be riding south around dawn tomorrow, then, Billy. You and I could link up a little further on.'

Billy nodded. 'That being so, I'll go and make a few preparations. I guess I'll leave town tonight and pick you up as you make tracks in the morning.'

They shook hands and parted.

11

Around seven-fifteen the following morning, Billy Bartram broke camp two miles south of Cochise Creek and converged upon the direction of Sandy East, who was riding hard and anxious to put a few miles between himself and the county seat before the opposition began to show itself.

It was half-past eight when they came together, and during the rest of the morning, their conversation was fleeting and almost non-existent. They camped for an hour in the heat of the day, and then went on again. That first day, when they only encountered one small settlement between towns, they rode until seven in the evening.

Their topics round the fire had to do with how far the opposition was away from them, and how the soil underfoot was gradually becoming more and more sandy. Billy had one question which he did not ask. Uppermost in his mind was a need to know how far Sandy was prepared to ride in a southerly direction before contemplating a change of plan.

Sandy appeared to be withdrawn into himself. But he was a good and efficient partner for a man to have between towns. The sharing of watches through the night gave them no difficulty. The second day's ride took them over almost as many miles.

After the brief midday rest, Billy hung back to try and find out the latest concerning the pursuers. From the first high tree which they had encountered that day, he perceived through his glass that Raymore and Della were now travelling with Long John and his boys.

The girl had discarded her woman's clothes in favour of a man's white shirt, denims and half boots. Her hair showed beneath a wide-brimmed grey hat like a copper curtain. She was riding a roan mare. Nils Raymore, mounted on a stockingfoot sorrel, was still her close companion, but even seen at a distance through a spyglass there was tension between Nils and some of the other men. Billy figured that they were vying for her attention, and as she was a very attractive young woman, he could not blame them.

The deputy sheriff caught up in a half hour and reported what he had seen. Sandy heard. He was excited and troubled. His anxiety showed during the second half of the day. About five o'clock, they rode into a cluster of adobes. Almost everyone who lived in this little settlement was Mexican.

They were friendly enough. Water was produced, and the horses were groomed while the two riders were given a hastily cooked meal and a few glasses of wine.

This cluster of dwellings was right in the heart of the border country. No one knew exactly where the border was, and no one seemed to care. Occasionally, the Mexican *rurales* rode through the village, and perhaps a little more rarely there were visits from the Arizona Rangers.

No questions were asked about the business of the visitors and no information was given. In a little over half an hour, the riding partners left again. Obviously, Sandy, who was doing the leading over this arid terrain, had some scheme in his mind. Billy knew that he would explain, if he thought words were necessary.

All through their travelling the bulking northern masses of the Sierra Madre Mountains were to eastward and the south. They remained tantalisingly for away. The ground became gritty, as though there was more rock in the area. This became evident in the last two hours of riding time that day. The growing thirst of riders and horses marked the time when Sandy usually called a halt.

Billy was on the point of asking why they were still going on on two occasions, but he restrained himself. As he waited and watched, there was a fairly quick change in the quality of the soil. Patches of green grass appeared where before there had only been sand and grit.

Billy began to smile, as shrubs and then trees which needed water began to show across their route. 'There's a waterway up ahead, an' you didn't bother to tell me!' he grumbled.

Sandy chuckled. 'It's a creek of the Yaqui river which runs out in the Gulf of California a long way south. I guess we'll camp near it. I thought the few extra miles might make it worth while, although there are times when it's almost a trickle in these parts.'

'Show me a trickle an' I'll be happy,' Billy promised.

He gave the dun a mild touch of the rowels and marvelled at the amount of energy it still had in its sweating body. The foliage on either side of the water was nowhere in any great depth, but it did transpose the landscape into one of some attractiveness.

They did not pull up until they were

through the bankside trees and the horses were ankle deep in water quenching their thirst.

Billy studied the position of the sun. 'I guess we ought to cross over. It would be safer that way, wouldn't it?'

Sandy nodded. 'There's a shallower spot about five or six hundred yards further west, but I figure these horses could manage the crossin' here all right.'

Again, they were in agreement. After slaking their own thirst and washing some of the perspiration off their bodies, they slackened their saddles and took the mounts across. Sandy was the first out of the water. He pointed to a well-grassed slope facing down towards the stream.

'How about building a camp fire about halfway up there, amigo?'

'You want they should know exactly where we are, Sandy?'

'Sure, I've got another little dodge up my sleeve. Maybe we can make capital out of it.'

170

Billy was happy to fall in with the suggestion. He built the fire in a fairly prominent position, and when he had it burning well, he went in search of his partner. To the south-west of the slope there was a thin belt of timber. It had been thicker a few years earlier, before some fleeting visitors had chopped down about half the boles with the idea of making a cabin of sorts.

A single log wall had been constructed, but since the builders had moved on to other parts, the wall had fallen down and remained in that position.

'We could use that as a raft, if the occasion arose,' Billy opined. 'Is that what you had in mind, Sandy?'

'Sure. I thought they might let us alone if they knew our whereabouts. Then we could slip downstream on a raft and save the stamina of our horses. This is definitely the last waterway where we're goin'. What do you think?'

'It's a good scheme, if we can get it to the water's edge, an' if the pursuit don't come too close tonight. So let's try it, huh?'

★   ★   ★

Bacon and a can of beans went down well with strong coffee. After about an hour, it was possible to catch glimpses of the oncoming pursuit through the spyglass at the top of the slope. The camp was just sufficiently distant across the water to make sniping difficult; not that the two partners expected any of that sort of trouble. At present, they were far too valuable to the opposition just pointing the way.

Billy acted as principal observer. He came back a half hour after dusk with a puzzled frown upon his face. Sandy, squatting upon the fallen log wall, glanced up, his face full of enquiry.

'They didn't settle where we expected them to, Sandy. When they saw our fire, instead of comin' straight on they altered direction to take them further westward. It's my belief they'll be quite close to

172

the stream, and maybe that shallow part you spoke about. I've been wondering how this fits in with your earlier plan.'

Sandy flicked a spur wheel and pushed his hat forward.

'Do you think we could move this raft to the water's edge? I mean without drawing too much attention to the manoeuvre.'

'I reckon we could, if it's still a good thing to do. If we waited a while, we might still slip past them unnoticed. Probably the stream turns south in a little while. Am I right?'

'Sure you're right. So let's rest up until dusk. Then we'll make our move.'

Sandy was sounding confident again, and this pleased Billy.

★　★　★

No one from the other camp attempted to come close. The log wall was heavy, but they succeeded in moving it by using the strength of both horses backed by themselves using poles as levers. The dun and the buckskin were almost belly deep in water by the time the pulling was over for them. Billy waded in and hauled them out again. He left them to Sandy's supervision, while he himself turned his attention to the fashioning of two long steering oars. Around eleven o'clock at night the two of them professed themselves ready to start on their rather risky venture.

Sandy started to say: 'If anything happens — '

'Don't worry, Sandy, I came along of my own accord. Besides, I elected to be a peace officer, nobody forced me to do the work. So let's relax and consider the next problems.'

They had a further short discussion, and as a result of that, Billy walked the two horses on to the raft and held them there, while Sandy worked a long lever to finally slip the crude raft away from the bank. Both of them were covered in perspiration by the time they had achieved their purpose, and the two horses were spooked a little when the raft rocked.

It soon became apparent that poling and steering a raft was not going to prove one of Sandy's strong points. He was eager and ready to give over his occupation to Billy as soon as the offer came. By that time they were shooting towards the danger area at a fairly fast speed.

'Do we attempt to return their fire, in the event they spot us and open up?' Sandy enquired hoarsely.

'I don't think they will, but we can be ready. It'll be vitally important to prevent the horses from plunging overboard if the alarm is raised,' Billy pointed out.

At that point, the partners became so quiet that they could distinctly hear the sound of the current working beneath them.

★　★　★

There was dissension in the enemy camp. It affected Long John, Lofty

Raymore, Jack Drex, Miff Thorn, and Della and Nils Raymore. From the start, the lesser members of the outlaw gang had respected the special relationship between Della and Nils, but Long John's interest in the woman showed more and more as the trek continued. Russ Blankers was aware of the Boss's interest in the woman, and he took every opportunity to foster it. Blankers' little tricks could only fester the wound of jealousy in Nils' heart.

On that evening, Nils had been selected to do the first lookout after dusk. He saw why this had been. He was to be out of the way while the men besported themselves round the campfire and enjoyed Della's company to the full.

Della had used her womanly wiles to great advantage since the party left Cochise Creek. Almost everyone in the group had, or thought he had, received a significant glance or two from the pretty widow.

Nils had taken to studying her, even

when they were riding side by side and the rest were well ahead or in the rear. He was vastly dissatisfied with the way things were going. On the only occasion when he had mentioned his dissatisfaction to her, she had laughed in his face and reminded him that he had introduced her to Long John: that the meeting had not been at her request.

Hence, Nils' black mood as he waited within a stone's throw of the water, and heard the happy goings on at the campfire, where a man was playing a mouth harp and the others were laughing and singing. He was away from them, and his absence was not noticed. Particularly was it not noticed by Della Rhodes. He was very bitter about Della's apparent growing in-difference to him, after travelling hundreds of miles as his sole companion.

He began to feel that with her it was only the pull of the loot taking her along, and that he — Nils — was only a means to that end. She wanted to be rich, but his company was not necessary. He was so steeped in misery that the overloaded raft almost slipped by unnoticed.

He blinked, pushed back his hat and focused his glass upon the water. Hidden by drooping waterside trees, he had a vantage point of great value. Not much light got into the spyglass, but he saw enough to know that Sandy East and Billy Bartram, the man with whom he had fought, were slipping by on the raft and taking their horses with them.

No unnecessary sound came from the scudding raft as it skimmed by slightly nearer the further bank. Even the horses behaved as though they had been schooled for this particular venture.

Nils watched the raft come level with his position. If he did his job properly, he was supposed to give the alarm without delay. While he thought about his present commitment, the whole company around the campfire let out a huge burst of laughter. Della's melodious voice, pitched higher than the others, twisted the knife of jealousy in his body.

She cried: 'Oh, John, that certainly is the funniest tale I've heard since I left Texas! I can hardly believe it is wholly true, but you do it justice in the tellin' an' that's a fact.'

Others were quick to applaud their Boss's witticisms. Nils glanced unhappily towards the fire. When next he gave his attention to the stream the raft had slipped past and was fast becoming a blur in the background shadows near the next bend. An idea came to him. One which he would not have contemplated a day ago. Why shouldn't he cut out from the rest and follow up the route setters on his own?

It was true that his brother, Lofty, was one of the group around the fire, but Lofty had ridden with Carrick for a long time. He was completely and utterly under the Boss's thumb. If ever there came a showdown between Nils and the Boss, Lofty would side against his kin. That much was already clear.

Nils licked his lips again. He thought of all the loot the greedy people around the campfire hoped to have for themselves. They didn't deserve it. *He* was doing the work at this critical time. They were taking him for granted, and that, he decided, was their undoing.

There was still time before he was due to be relieved. His horse was to hand with the saddle slackly draped on its back. All he had to do was walk it away from the camp area, then mount up and go in pursuit of the two elusive men on the raft.

This time he acted, and no uncalled for sounds gave him away as he made the break.

12

It was a half hour after midnight when the jovial party around Long John's campfire began to give themselves over to yawns and thoughts of the bedroll. Jack Drex should have taken over as guard a whole half hour earlier, but he had relished a longer stay at the fire, thinking that Nils was alert and probably sulking by the stream.

Five minutes elapsed before the bald man came back and gave the rather startling news that Nils was no longer with them. Headed by Long John, the whole of the party tramped through the high grass and examined the place where the lookout had been posted.

The men eyed one another and then looked away. The two who felt most uncomfortable were Della and Lofty. The latter started to shake his head as speculative thoughts went through the minds of the party.

'Nils was always something of a mystery to me,' he remarked. 'Besides, I ain't really known him in the last year or two. Della could fill you boys in on a few details, I guess.'

The young woman stepped back a pace. Obviously, all the others thought that Nils had gone over to the other party — to Billy and her brother. Out there in the desert, men were apt to think the worst of their fellows without much provocation.

'Now see here, boys,' she said heatedly. 'Whatever Nils has done, he's acted on the spur of the moment. *I* don't know why he's done it, or what made him make a sudden change. Why don't you go over there an' see what the situation is at the other camp? If you ask me, there's something queer about that fire on the hill slope. It wouldn't surprise me if that tricky little brother of mine, an' his sidekick, have slipped away while we were all busy enjoyin' ourselves.'

The deep voice of Long John took over. 'Jack, you an' Miff slip over there an' get wise to the true situation. You don't have to make your presence known. Now get goin'. Maybe if you'd changed as guard at the proper time this wouldn't have happened.'

John had been suffering from a bad headache occasioned by the sun for part of the day. Now, his tone suggested that this bad humour had returned.

The crossing of Drex and Thorn was a noisy affair. Long before they made the other side, it became clear to the watchers on the bank that the two young riding partners had moved on under cover of darkness. Thorn was the one who actually went up the slope and did the shouting.

No one answered him when he made his revelations. Jack Drex was too disgusted to tell him to be quiet. Drex started back alone. The site of the cabin which had never been erected remained undiscovered. Fifteen uneasy minutes later, the party assembled at the smouldering fire and discussed what to do.

Blankers fingered his beard. His gaze was averted from Della and Long John as he said his piece. 'If Nils is out of sorts with the rest of us, he may go over to the other two and suggest some sort of a deal, excluding the rest of us. First and foremost, he will do his best to have them ride at a greater speed. So maybe we ought to consider putting a few more miles behind us before we bed down.'

In the semi-desert area such a suggestion could only meet with a disappointed reaction.

Della murmured: 'I'll go along with whatever you men decide. Don't hold back on account of me. I can take it.' Her eyes were on the shadowy face of Long John as she spoke.

'All right, so we'll saddle up an' ride for maybe a couple of hours, folks,' John suggested. 'Get your things together. The sooner we get started the sooner we bed down again. So let's hit the leather, an' keep your eyes skinned as you go this time.'

He panned a significant glance around his minions. They knew he was hinting at possible treachery from Nils Raymore.

★   ★   ★

Around three o'clock the following morning, Billy and the Kid were stretched out in their blankets on opposite sides of a low Apache-style fire on the east side of the Yaqui creek some five miles further south. They had been turned in long enough to be in a deep sleep when the stirring of the two horses, pegged out a few yards away, brought them back to wakefulness.

Only a few seconds separated their coming awake.

'What is it, Billy?' the Kid asked.

'Sounds like we've got a visitor, after all. He must have come along the bank and seen the raft. I wonder who it is?'

Sandy scowled. 'If seeing the raft

brought him across the creek, then he must have seen it before. He must have seen it go by! If he's alone, he must have been their guard. Maybe we ought to get ready to receive him.'

The discussion went on in whispers for a few seconds more. Then all was still again around the fire. Raymore left his mount by the river bank and advanced on foot. He stood looking at the peaceful scene for over a minute from fifty feet away. As far as he could tell his arrival was unnoticed. He was squaring his shoulders and boosting his morale over this consideration when a horse suddenly came to its feet and startled him.

The unexpected voice of Billy Bartram called out: 'You've been following me for rather a long way, Raymore. Surely you didn't come all this way to see what I look like in a bedroll?'

'Shucks, Bartram, did you know I was here all the time?'

Raymore stepped forward rather carefully, holding out his hands to show that he had no weapons in them. Sandy yawned, threw aside his blanket, and dropped a revolver down beside him.

'Some folks sure do pick awkward times to do their visitin' an' that's for sure!' he remarked. 'Did you bring a message, or did you come of your own accord?'

The new arrival stepped between them, glanced from one to another and cautiously boosted the fire. He straightened up, still not quite sure about his reception. Billy then brought his hands above his blanket and put down his Colt. This action further surprised Raymore, and then gave him the confidence to go on.

'I saw your raft go by, but I didn't tell anybody. I came of my own accord because I thought I might be of use to you. Do you want me to go on?'

'Take the weight off your legs an' say your piece,' Billy suggested brusquely.

'You don't sound all that friendly,' Raymore complained, 'but maybe that's understandable — '

'Four men have died since I started to take an interest in the affairs of Sandy East, so don't expect a big welcome, brother. Come to think of it, the number is five, not four. Now, why are you here an' what do you want? Remember that sleep is precious, and we're only cool for a few hours.'

Billy really sounded like a veteran lawman as he administered this rebuke to Nils Raymore. The latter frowned, but when Sandy offered no comment, he went on.

'Back there you have Long John, Russ Blankers, Drex, Thorn, my brother Lofty, an' Sandy's sister, Della. They've banded together on account of they're interested in the loot you're supposed to be travellin' towards.'

'Tell us something we don't know,' Sandy protested quietly.

'Hell an' tarnation, I'm here to do you a favour,' Raymore protested. 'There's only two of you, surely you could use an extra gun? Three's better than two any day. That's the way *I* see it!'

'So you came ahead jest to do us a favour, Raymore?' Billy resumed, from the shadowy depths of his bedroll. 'Are you sure you didn't leave the others to help yourself?'

Raymore groaned. 'All right, so put it that way, if you like. Della is payin' attention to Long John, an' I'm feelin' out of things. I wanted to quit the group, go over to the opposition. I can't rightly figure why you ain't keen to see me. I could have sneaked up on you with my guns drawn, if I'd felt like it.'

'Any such move on your part, an' you'd be corpse number six,' Sandy pointed out calmly. 'Incidentally, if you've come over to us hopin' for a big reward, I wouldn't count on it. We might be spared by your old buddies because we are supposed to know the location of something very valuable. In your case, you might be shot out of hand, as a turncoat. Have you considered that?'

'Eh, well, yes, I suppose I have,' Raymore replied unhappily. 'But you *do* know where the loot is, don't you?'

Sandy yawned again. 'I know where it *was*, but that was some time ago, amigo. A whole lot of people might be disappointed on this trip. Why don't you think over the situation an' then decide whether you'd like to ride with us? We won't hold it against you if you've pulled out by the time we break camp.'

A few seconds elapsed, during which Raymore scrambled to his feet. He licked his lips thirstily, but no one suggested he should take coffee. He murmured something about going for a walk up the bank, to think things over.

Out of the encroaching darkness, after the visitor had gone, Sandy said: 'Do you think he'll go, or stay?'

'It's hard to tell,' Billy opined. 'He might jest try to put one over on us in order to get back in favour with his old pardners. Maybe we ought to sleep the rest of the night with one eye open.'

Sandy approved this course of action.

He added: 'I didn't like what he said about Della. Her takin' up with Long John, an' all.'

Billy grunted sympathetically. 'Maybe she had no alternative, Sandy. After all, she's in this mess pretty deep now.'

The night silence finally took charge again. They slept fitfully. Half an hour after Raymore started back in the direction of the Carrick camp, the dense shadow of a pair of lush trees suddenly sprouted a man on horseback.

A voice said: 'Halt!'

Raymore obeyed at once. In the space of a few seconds he had learned a lot. Even in the gloom, the horse could be seen to have a white coat. The Quaker-style hat gave away the identity of the tall, straight-backed figure in the saddle. And the deep, fruity, authoritative voice of the rider could only have belonged to one man — Carrick!

Nils had been thinking a lot since the pair out in front had more or less refused his friendship and help. Now, as he was taken by surprise by the one man whom he would have guessed would be sleeping, he tried out his excuses.

'Long John! Fancy you prowlin' about on your own like this! By the way, this is Nils, Nils Raymore. I was on guard duty, but something came up an' I thought I ought to follow it out without givin' the alarm! Would you believe it, East and his sidekick actually went past our camp on a log raft!'

The restless white stallion closed the gap with the sorrel. Carrick was seen to be holding a revolver close in to his body. His ill-assorted eyes were completely unreadable in the darkness. Most of the menace came through his voice.

'Why did you come back, Nils?' Carrick asked flatly.

'To report to you, of course! Ain't I been one of your outfit since Cochise Creek? I wanted to tell you what they were doing. Now, I'm here. All I want to do is give up my information! Do you doubt me?'

Raymore put a lot of effort into the way he said the words about doubting. Carrick did not give an answer to that, one way or the other.

'What else did you find out?'

'They're camped on the other bank, maybe two or three miles further south. The raft is there, right by them. They appear to be in good shape, an' headin' straight for the place where the loot is cached.'

'Did they tell you that?'

'Well no, not in so many words. East seemed to be hedgin'. He tried to make me believe that the treasure might have been moved by somebody else, since it was buried. But I didn't take the least bit of notice of that. You wouldn't have expected me to, would you?'

'Anything else?' Carrick prompted, unfeelingly.

'Nothin' special, Boss. I didn't get all that close, you see,' Raymore protested quietly.

The head under the big flat hat nodded. A moment later, the steady

193

revolver was fired twice, at a distance where it would have been hard to miss. Both bullets hit Raymore in the chest. He stiffened and fell sideways out of the saddle, almost at once.

Carrick snorted. He dismounted, glanced towards the river to see how far the bank was away, and moved around to examine his victim. The eyes were just glazing over as he bent down. John picked up Raymore by the shoulders, dragged him over to the water's edge, and launched him.

Breathing hard, the renegade chief straightened up. He started to think that he was far less fit than he had been two years ago. Penitentiary food, hard physical work over long hours, and now the punishment which hot semi-arid country metes out to white men had taken their toll. He omitted frequent spells of riotous living and a big intake of alcohol and nicotine from his calculations.

He was glad to lean against a tree bole before mounting up again and returning to his minions with the sorrel in tow.

Fifty yards south of their new camp, Blankers and Drex came out to meet him. They saw the stockingfoot, noted that it was riderless and at once assumed what had happened.

Long John rode on, into the midst of the others, before dismounting and standing back with his back to the fire. Della rose to her feet and stood before him enquiringly, with a blanket closely wrapped round her. Lofty Raymore stood at the back of the group, tugging at his black tuft of chin beard and pretending that he was no more concerned than the others.

'I found him, folks,' John announced calmly. 'Or rather he found me. He was hidden up in the bushes alongside of the water. He presented me with the muzzle of his gun an' said I'd been interferin' too much in his life lately.

'I tried to talk him out of it, but he wouldn't listen an' when I was certain he was goin' to blast me out of the saddle, I risked a quick draw an' beat him to it. In daylight I wouldn't have stood a chance. My bullets were on the mark. I figure he died instantly. His body slipped into the water, an' that was the last I saw of him. I'm kind of sorry for those of you who knew him better than I did, but the heat of the border country does things to people. Maybe it turned his head, or something. Me, I ain't been feelin' too well myself.

'Right now, I think we all ought to turn in. No need for a lookout this time. Sooner or later, we'll pick up the sign we want to find. So let's hit the blanket.'

John yawned hugely. He drank half a cup of lukewarm coffee and turned towards his bedroll. Della's roll was right beside him. He thought she looked something special with her long copper-coloured hair spilled out over her saddle, showing red highlights in the glow from the fire.

'How are you feelin', John?' Della murmured, when the others had bedded down.

'Kind of weary, Della, but a few hours' sleep should restore me. Besides, I've got prospects. That vision of a rich and settled existence is still vivid in the mind. An' if it's comin' to me, it shouldn't be far off.'

The young woman chuckled. 'Patience is all that is wanted now, John. Patience and a little luck.'

Her eyes were fixed on the Boss's shadowy face until his stertorous breathing made it clear that he was asleep.

13

Within an hour of the recommence-
ment of their journey, Sandy East made
a decided turn towards the east, riding
into a fertile valley, which was fringed
and cushioned by the furthest north of
the foothills of the bulky Mexican
Sierra Madre.

The heat continued to take its toll of
them and their horses, but what lay
ahead was a source of great curiosity to
Billy, who focused his spyglass upon it,
and picked out details too far away for
the human eye.

He said: 'You've been here before,
Sandy. If you'd asked me, an' I really
did go to school for a year or two, I'd
have said that there was no settlement
of any kind in this part of the border
belt.'

Sandy laughed heartily. He, too,
seemed to be just as interested in the

settlement ahead. 'They call it Border-ville. No one is really sure whether it is in the United States, or in Mexico. You'll recollect from your history lessons that this stretch of country once belonged to Mexico, an' that it was purchased by the American government in 1853. Called the Gadsden Purchase.

'You'll find out when we get there that the folks don't much mind whether they're in Mexico, or the United States. They're kind of different from any other community I've come across.'

Billy nodded. Presently, squinting through the glass made his eye ache and he collapsed it and put it away.

'Tell me one thing. Are there any more settlements before we get to the area of the 'dig'?'

'No more at all,' Sandy answered definitely. 'I guess you wonder why I've come this far, drawin' the outlaws along behind us. Well, there's a reason, as you'll see shortly. I get drawn this way, but not for the same reasons as the Carrick outfit. Besides, I'd say all differences between us and them will be realised in the next couple of days. You'll be able to go back then to your ordinary job.'

Billy wanted to remark that he could only return if he was in one piece, but he thought such a remark to be ill-timed, so he did not utter it.

Gradually, the township ahead took their whole interest. There appeared to be two races, the white Americans and the darker-skinned Mexicans, and all were well and truly mixed. On a slight downgrade, various forms of manual endeavour could be seen and identified.

For instance, upwards of two score Mexicans were working in a walled-off area which was taking the shape of a vineyard. In another direction, Americans were building a windmill. A mixed group of both races were concentrating hard on the digging of a well.

The buildings were mostly houses, as might have been expected. There was no rigid distinction between Mexican adobes and American log and board cabins. Streets were there, but the buildings had been put up without any particular attempt at order. Shacks and adobes were well and truly mixed.

Four men in denims were working on the roof of a squat church with a bell tower. Other men, toiling at a greater distance, were building a wooden place of worship with the beginning of a lean steeple.

Billy marvelled that there was so much industry in such a hot, unknown place. He was just saying as much to Sandy when some of the labourers in the vineyard straightened their backs and recognised the blue-eyed youth mounted on the buckskin horse.

'Ah, Senor Sandy! How good it is to see you back with us!' a stout, beaming man called.

'And you have brought a friend with you, too!' another remarked.

'*Buenos dias, amigos!*' Sandy called. He lifted his hat and waved it as the whole work force straightened up and gave him a cordial welcome.

Billy was so moved by the demonstration of friendship that he lifted his own hat and held it across his chest until the vineyard had gone by. A boy with a team of mules pulled in to the side of the street and waved a straw hat to them. This same boy went off up the street and spread the exciting news of their arrival.

Workers, both men and women, came from the buildings and clustered round their horses, patting their rumps and grinning up into the riders' faces.

'This time, you have come to stay, Senor Sandy? Where is your friend, Senor Red?'

Young East was beginning to shrug about whether he could stay permanently, but the reference to Red Murdo hardened his expression.

'I am afraid my friend, Red, is dead. He met with an accident, amigos. But it is good to be back among you, even without him. Greetings to you and your families.'

A gentle clamour of returned greetings welled up from the crowd. The two new arrivals remained as they were, ringed in by friendly faces, until three men of some importance pushed their way to the front and took the riders' attention. Sandy at once dismounted. Billy remained where he was for another minute or so, studying the newcomers. He had a feeling of strange unreality, as if he had ridden into another world.

These three men obviously had the authority in the town. The most striking figure was that of a clergyman in a brown monk-like habit. He had a lean, ascetic face, and his greying thin hair had been shaved off all over his skull. A flat, wide-brimmed hat shadowed his black brows and the rather intense wideset eyes beneath them.

The tall man with the stethoscope draped round his neck had a lean, lined face. He wore the trousers and buttoned vest of a grey suit which had seen better days. He was six feet tall and walked with a limp. His black stetson was crumpled rather than carefully dented.

The last of the trio was another tall man, but he was by far the youngest, being around thirty years of age. He was bare-headed, although his thick brown hair and floppy quiff gave him scarcely adequate protection from the sun. His eyes had an intense, almost wild look, such as in some men denotes fanaticism. He had been working hard, and was still blowing out his hollow cheeks when the meeting took place. His clerical collar and white shirt were grimy with toil. He was a man who had triumphed over lung trouble in the border climate.

Sandy shook hands warmly with all three. He gestured towards Billy. 'Gentlemen, I want you to meet my friend, Billy Bartram. Red is dead, following an accident. Billy, here, is a deputy sheriff, but he is in sympathy with me and only professionally interested in my enemies.'

Billy at once dismounted and offered his hand to the trio. He was introduced in turn to Father Ignatius, Doctor Jefferson Scott, and to the Reverend David Myett. All of them suggested quite warmly that he was welcome to Borderville.

Jefferson Scott, M.D., was the one to lead them away to his house, which was on the far side of the church with the bell tower. All five of them assembled in his living-room, and sat down to a glass of wine around a table covered with a smart green cloth. Two pot plants gave the room a nice atmosphere, and someone cooking food in another part of the house was quietly singing a Spanish song.

'You've made much progress since I was here last, my friends,' Sandy observed.

Each of the three residents had a piece to say in return, but Billy was only half listening. He was entranced by the change in his young companion. Sandy seemed many years older than his real age when he talked to these men, and this was to two who were old enough to be his father.

They talked to him as though they had great faith in him, and as if he possessed wisdom beyond his years. After a few minutes' talk, Father Ignatius spread his hands.

'Sandy, it is good to see you in our midst again, an' your friend Billy is most welcome. Forgive us if we have to ask this, but when you went away you had decided to stay in the land of your birth. We are wondering what brought about this change in you, and whether you are really in need of a lawman friend.'

Sandy nodded, and lowered his eyes to the cloth. He toyed with his wine glass.

'Friends, I was forced to change my plans on account of the greed of others. I have trouble on my back trail. Our enemies will be along this way before many hours have passed. Leading them will be a man named Long John

Carrick, not long out of the penitentiary. He is after considerable wealth, which he proposes to use as the basis of his future income. He wants to retire and live the life of a rich man. The others with him are probably as greedy.'

Billy shot him a quick glance, knowing that he was including his own sister.

'The townsfolk will fight. We still have weapons, even if we don't show them,' Dr Scott pointed out.

'You should know that there is a woman with this pursuing party,' Billy put in, 'and she is Sandy's own sister. She is probably misguided, but the ties of the blood are still there.'

Grave nods from the three local listeners. After a silence, the Reverend Myett's impatience moved him to words. 'But you would want our community to fight, to preserve our way of life, an' to protect you, Sandy?'

'We can stop them and turn them back, Sandy, as you well know,' Father Ignatius added.

'Not without a lot of bloodshed,' Sandy argued. 'It will be best to let them come through. Let them follow me and my pardner. Borderville must be protected. You know how things stand. A thriving young community can hardly get off to a good start if its streets have to run with blood first.'

Father Ignatius made a steeple of the fingers of his two hands.

'Sandy, you are wise beyond your years, but in allowing these enemies of society to come through we will be putting you in grave danger. You know what the outcome is likely to be, but does your friend? Can we ask him to chance his life in the same way?'

Sandy slowly turned his head towards Billy. He stared frankly at him, knowing him well and yet wondering what his reaction would be to this question.

Billy licked his lips. 'As a deputy sheriff I don't hate my fellow men. Only these who follow are sufficiently evil for me to want them dead. If they overtake us an' are not satisfied with what they find, our lives would be in jeopardy. But I've known that all along. So don't worry on my behalf. Havin' seen this town of yours, Borderville, I'll go along with what Sandy has said. I say show the renegades the way, if necessary. We'll be prepared.'

The surviving Coyote Kid gave Billy a warm smile. He nodded to the others, as though to say 'I told you so'. They in turn showed mild but sincere approval. At that point, the meeting broke up.

While a meal was being prepared, Sandy took his partner on a tour of the town, accompanied by the doctor. The parson's son was impressed with everything, but he had one burning question which he had to ask when the tour was finished.

'Tell me, Doc, how does the town flourish? Everybody works, but no one has yet come along from the outside world to buy your produce an' such. How do you get the wherewithal to live?'

'That's a shrewd question, young fellow. Sandy, here, knows the answer. Maybe if you survive what lies ahead of you and get back here in one piece, he'll let you into the secret.'

Billy stuck a boot up on the gallery of the doctor's house. He grinned at his two friends. 'So, the knowledge is to be a reward for survival, is it? All right, I'll go along with that. Whatever it is that makes this place tick, it sure is worth while.'

The doctor and the Kid exchanged a brief but significant glance. Billy was more than ever intrigued. He marvelled at the change in atmosphere from that which Carrick's outfit carried around with them. In the midst of the townsfolk of Borderville, it was hard to believe that the renegade gang was so far out of touch with the rest of society.

Over the next meal, the discussion was about moving on again.

14

In the early afternoon, when the town had gone quiet on account of siesta, Billy and Sandy were left to rest in a cool room in the doctor's house. On their own, their thoughts went back to the hard riding of the past few days.

The Kid was restless, and Billy also found it hard to sleep. Presently Sandy's impatience outgrew that of his friend. He raised himself up on an elbow and called to Billy, who answered promptly.

'I feel we ought to move on, Billy. I don't rightly know why but I wouldn't like to be overhauled in this town by the Carrick outfit.'

'Oddly enough, I have the same sort of feeling,' Billy confessed. He had a suggestion to make. 'How would it be if we split up for an hour or two? I'd like to ride back a mile or so, and see if I can lead the gang astray. It might be possible for them to miss Borderville altogether. What do you think?'

'You think it would be good if they missed the town?' Sandy queried.

'I certainly do, Sandy, an' so do you. I can see it in your face. Why don't you ride on a mile or two, an' I'll catch you up? After all, many folks in this town seem to know where you're goin' an' they can direct me.'

Sandy was slow to agree to this plan. His slowness made the deputy impatient. He showed his mood and the Kid tried to explain his doubts.

'You might be forced into action. If you had to retreat to Bordersville the outlaws would enter with drawn guns, an' many innocent people might have to suffer.'

'I'll try not to do anything foolish,' Billy promised, and with that agreement was reached.

Some forty minutes later, Billy was well up the slope to westward of the new town, while Sandy was leaving it by another route to go further south. The deputy pushed his big dun horse rather hard as a fairly high spot in the terrain loomed up ahead. Through the last of the trees on the near side of the slopes, he found himself breathless with excitement.

Suddenly he was at the top and reining back to hold the dun in check. He gasped in surprise, for there, right below him were the riders he had expected. Just a few hundred yards separated him from the strung-out line. Even while he looked, two men saw him and pointed forward. If he expected a sudden gallop on horseback, he was to be disappointed.

He swung the dun about, still undecided what to do. However, he had come along in the hope of distracting them from a visit to the new town, and if he was to effect his self-imposed mission, he would have to act quickly. He remembered the gravity of Sandy's last discussion with him, and hoped that he was not about to precipitate trouble, as he pulled his Winchester.

Hurriedly putting it to his shoulder, he fired off two rapid shots over the heads of the men riding on the rugged southern flank of the group. As the echoes faded, their shouts were audible. Two men broke away from the main body. One of them had a lot of beard, and was obviously Blankers. The other man's face also ran to facial hair. The hirsute ones were acting in this operation.

Waving his weapon like an Indian on the warpath, Billy turned the dun towards the foothills further south. Blankers and Raymore broke away to follow him. They fired a couple of ranging shots to keep him on the move and took up the chase. Billy and the dun swept clear of all cover about one hundred yards further down the slope. As he rode clear, he glanced back, and to his surprise he found that the opposition had slowed. One of them, Blankers, was using a spyglass. The sun was glinting on the lens.

Billy slowed up, threw up his weapon and fired at the bearded man. To his surprise, this provocation failed to bring a renewal of the chase. Raymore gave him what appeared to be a rude gesture. This was repeated by Blankers. After that, the two outlaws turned their horses about and went back the way they had come.

Frustrated and angry, Billy knew that he had failed in his purpose. Only two of the party had followed him, and as soon as *they* had seen who he was they had given up the chase. Obviously, in their eyes, he was small fry compared with the Kid. And what was more, the main party was apparently heading straight for the town.

Muttering to himself, Billy brought the dun back to a fine turn of speed, Now, he was determined to return to town ahead of the newcomers, and to give the warning before leaving again to rejoin his riding partner.

The going which he had chosen was rough, but before he actually came up

215

with the town he encountered Doc Scott, sitting a horse in trees. The medical man now had a Colt strapped low on his right thigh, and he certainly looked as if he knew how to use it. He saw Billy's meaningful glance.

'You don't like the idea of a sawbones toting guns, huh?' he muttered, with a grimace. 'Well, let me tell you, you young whipper-snapper of a badge toter, there have been countless occasions in my career when I've had to defend my patients from the lawless.'

'You mean before you came to Borderville?' Billy asked innocently.

'I didn't say that, but it's the truth, anyway. So now you've failed to turn away these carrion, an' you want to return to your pardner? That's the way it should be. I'll see to the alarm in town. How good are you at readin' signs?'

Without waiting for Billy to reply, the doctor started to give directions for a link-up with Sandy which did not involve going into town. After a brief handshake, the frustrated young man rode off in the direction of a bulking outcrop towards the south-east. The frowning peaks of the Sierra Madre reared up much higher behind it, but there was a world of sky and sun between the two landmarks.

★   ★   ★

Around five o'clock, Billy cleared a spur of the foothills well south of Borderville and started away from the high ground in a direction he believed to be due south. Within fifteen minutes, he had overtaken the Kid, who was resting behind the largest of a scattering of three huge rocks, a good furlong away on the plateau.

The greeting was a brief but cordial one. Sandy eyed his friend quizzically.

'It didn't work out the way I wanted it,' Billy admitted. 'They were closer to the town than I thought. I tried to draw them away to the south. For a short time, Blankers an' another came after me, but then they got to seein' me through a spyglass an' they lost interest.'

Billy sounded outraged, and Sandy found time to smile at him.

'So they rode straight into town, did they? Obviously I'm the one they're after. But don't fret about the failure of your plan. You meant well, and that means an awful lot accordin' to the folks of Borderville.'

Billy did not look as if he derived much comfort from Sandy's words. Nor did he have anything further to say when Sandy suggested that they should ride for at least another couple of hours before camping for the night.

The terrain was harsh, being mostly sandy. There were rocks scattered about, but few sizeable enough to give shelter to the travellers. Horses and men suffered from the protracted heat and the reflected dazzle of bright sunlight. They were dry and irritable when Sandy pointed out yet another cluster of hot, dry rock, and said that it would do for their night spot.

The Kid made himself quite busy within the ring of rocks. He seemed almost cheerful as he built the fire and produced canned goods and a skinful of extra water. By comparison, Billy looked overtired and out of sorts with himself. The sun had drained him of a lot of body salt, in perspiration.

'How far is the actual spot we're headed for?' Billy asked bluntly, as he lay stretched out on the warm sand, chest downwards, with a thin smoke between his fingers.

'We'll make it tomorrow,' Sandy promised. 'Tomorrow things will resolve themselves. We'll see the outcome and everything else a whole lot clearer.'

'If that's so, then tonight is important, an' I insist on takin' the first watch. We'll make it three hours. What do you say?'

Young East was very thoughtful. He was slow to answer, but when he did, he agreed. For a time, they rested, watching the sharp shadows which the rocks made as the sun dipped down in the west. After a time, the growing darkness blended the dark patches with the growing greyness. Shortly after that, they knew that the sun was down. This knowledge made them edgy.

Billy had a feeling that he was out of his depth, beyond his normal range. He kept staring at Sandy's bedroll when the latter had curled up to sleep. He was wondering what it would be like in these remote parts to be entirely alone.

Every half hour during his watch, he rose up from the side of the fire and prowled around the rocks which protected them. Few living creatures shared the desert with them. A restless herd of cows would have been comfort of a sort. Billy tried to take his mind off his loneliness by projecting his thoughts back home.

He was still visualising the island on which his father lived when Sandy came and shook him by the shoulder.

'Time for you to turn in, amigo. You were dozing, but nothing's happened.

So bed down properly and get what sleep you can because the sun will be high again before we know it.'

'Okay, Sandy, wear your sheepskin vest 'cause it sure does go cold when the sun's down in these parts. It'll be almost daylight by the time you call me. Goodnight.'

★　★　★

Billy was asleep almost at once. The next thing he heard was the angry braying of a mule. He sat up with a jerk, blinking his eyes and getting ready to call to his partner, but the figure which crossed from the other side of the fire was tall with a tuft of chin beard. He also had a Colt revolver ready in his hand and pointing.

Lofty Raymore called: 'It's all over, Russ, I've got the other hombre right here. He was sleepin' like a babe. Such a pity to disturb him, it was. Darned if it ain't that young fellow who tried to make us come the wrong way before we found the town. Do you remember?'

Sandy East moved into the firelight with his hands raised. Directly behind him was Blankers, Carrick's top gun. And searching the camp area were Jack Drex and Miff Thorn.

Sandy murmured: 'I'm sorry for the way things have turned out, Billy. I've let you down.'

Blankers rumbled with laughter, deep in his barrel chest. He turned over the Kid to Thorn, and holstered his weapon. Billy gave the new arrivals the once over. Four men, four horses, and four mules.

'Carrick don't appear to be present, Sandy,' the deputy remarked. 'I'm surprised Long John let Blankers take charge of this outfit after what happened when Red Murdo was taken.'

'I'm a little surprised myself,' Sandy returned, 'but perhaps it's understandable. After all, the gang has lost a few men lately. It's goin' down in numbers as well as in talent.'

Blankers clipped him across the face

with the back of his hand.

'Jest don't get fresh with me, Kid. I ain't the type to put up with it. Red could have told you that, if he'd lived.'

Sandy went down on one knee and stayed there. The menace of Blankers was still there when Billy cleared his throat and spoke up.

'You ain't the type to make the same mistake twice, either, Blankers. If you mishandle East like you did Murdo, Carrick will be dispensin' with your services!'

Raymore, Drex and Thorn were taken aback by this bold talk. Blankers clenched his fists and fumed, but he knew that he had to keep a tight grip on himself at this stage. Bartram was right. He couldn't afford to slip up twice. Instead of raging on and making threats about torture, he stormed away from the spot and gave his attention to the mules.

When he returned, his minions were looking him over doubtfully. But he had made up his mind what to do. The prisoners were trussed and put down to rest fairly close to the fire. Lofty Raymore was put on guard, and warned to do it more efficiently than East had done.

The rest then turned in until dawn.

Sleep eluded Billy for a long time. He was wondering how Sandy had managed to stay asleep while four horses and four mules toiled up to their camping spot in the dead of night. He was still puzzled about his partner's apparent lapse when sleep claimed him again.

15

Oddly enough, both Sandy and Billy slept well, once they had managed to push pressing problems to the backs of their minds. The first rays of the sun were creeping slowly nearer to them when they awakened in the normal fashion.

Blankers was standing by the fire, which had been boosted for breakfast. Sticking out of a portion of the blaze was the handle of the branding iron which had been used to try and loosen Red Murdo's tongue.

Sandy eyed it speculatively, propped up on one elbow. He figured that the Carrick boys were due for a surprise when the cajolery began.

Lofty Raymore was walking around, chewing on a match stick. He looked first at the Kid and then at Billy Bartram. Drex and Thorn, although not quite so wide awake, stalked around behind him, and also gave a lot of attention to the prisoners.

Raymore said: 'Do you figure the East boy for a talkative hombre?'

Thorn grinned, but Drex shook his head. 'I don't figure he has much to say in the ordinary course of events. But folks do say he's mighty keen on his friends, so he might talk to save his pardner from trouble. I guess things will work out pretty soon, when Russ states his wants.'

Sandy yawned and took the attention of everyone. 'If you're heatin' up that iron to give one of your celebrated demonstrations, Blankers, don't bother. I'll show you where it is you want to go, an' you'll need all your strength for the ride and the dig. So how about loosening these bonds to help the circulation, because if you don't we won't be able to ride properly, an' I might lose my way.'

Blankers was nibbling his beard with his teeth. His eyebrows showed the kind of speculation which was going on in his head. While he watched, Sandy struggled to his feet, and gestured to Drex, the nearest outlaw, for a knife.

'All right, cut him loose, Jack. Cut 'em both loose,' Blankers ordered. 'After all, they've got no weapons, an' they ain't likely to get far if they make a break for it. An' come to think of it, I'm hungry, so let's have us a good breakfast.'

The whole party ate well, but there was little conversation over the food. Sandy spent a lot of time peering south through a glass, and occasionally studying the direction of the nearest spur of the Sierra Madre.

'How long will it take us to find the loot?' Raymore enquired, in a whisper.

'It's nearer than you think,' Sandy answered enigmatically.

★   ★   ★

The tops of the palm trees started to show directly south after two hours of steady endeavour across the gritty sand. Sandy was too intent upon the tree cluster for it to be other than the place they sought.

Billy, riding at his elbow, was as curious as the bunched outlaws riding along behind. 'Is there water at the oasis?' he asked.

'There was the last time I came this way, Billy. Here's hopin' it hasn't dried up in between times.'

This remark was overheard, and the renegades saw the small water hole after that as a doubly desirable haven. The horses were prompted to a greater effort, and even the mules put up a good speed without much goading. Exactly two hours more brought the perspiring group of riders almost to the oasis. In the last hundred yards before the inviting shade of a score or so of stunted palms, Blankers suddenly seemed to grow anxious. He put the spurs to his horse and forged ahead, almost as if he expected some sort of trap at the water-hole. He did not draw rein until the shadow of the trees was about him.

There was water for the asking further into the oasis, but he then checked his thirsty animal and eagerly awaited the arrival of his two prisoners. One came up on either side of him, closely flanked by the other riders.

Fixing his small, cunning eyes on the Kid, he asked: 'Is this the place where the loot is buried, or is it jest a stoppin' place for water?'

Sandy glanced around the other avid faces before answering.

'Everything you want is here. Take my advice and see to the needs of your men and their animals before you start looking for anything.'

Blankers began to fume, but before he could answer, the other three riders who had come along with him urged their horses towards the still pool in the centre. They dismounted and threw themselves down to stick their heads in the water. The horses, no longer needed as beasts of burden, moved a little way around the pool and cautiously sipped the contents.

'Well, the horses approve of it, so it must be pure,' Billy remarked, as he dismounted.

'Drink slowly, amigo,' Sandy advised, as he did the same.

The last to reach the water were the four mules, and they were shooed away to the other side while the various water canteens and the skin were replenished first. For upwards of five minutes, everyone was content to slake his thirst and counteract the excessive heat of the sun.

After that, men raised themselves on their elbows and eyed one another, glancing around the small confines of the water-hole and then at Sandy East.

'All right, East, where is it?' Blankers asked bluntly.

'You want to start digging straight away?' Sandy asked.

'Why should anybody want to delay? We're all losin' moisture an' we've come a long way to collect. Sure, we want to get started! Any reason why we shouldn't?'

Sandy shook his head. 'It'll take a long time if we don't all dig together 'cause it's buried deep. Send somebody to get all the spades and bring them over to the south-west corner.'

The Kid headed for his location spot with his friend alongside of him. Billy murmured: 'All the time, I've been after Carrick and his mob. I haven't changed at all, Sandy.'

'Be patient, you'll get your chance,' the Kid promised, in a whisper. And then in a louder voice: 'Here we are! See these three palms with a piece chipped out of the boles at head height. The burial spot is right in the middle of them.'

Raymore handed over a spade. Sandy took it and roughly marked out a rectangle with the blade. Without any ceremony he removed his sheepskin vest and began to dig at one corner. Billy availed himself of a tool and started to work in another corner. When prompted by Blankers, Drex and Thorn picked up spades and made it four working at once. The soil was quite sandy, and workable, but the heat of the sun made the effort painful.

The prisoners paused every few minutes, dripping with perspiration and needing water. Blankers paced the perimeter, muttering and encouraging the others to get a move on. Presently, Drex and Thorn dropped out. Their places were taken by Raymore and Blankers. The new pair started to work with feverish haste, but they soon slowed up.

'What exactly are we lookin' for?' Lofty asked hoarsely.

Sandy used the question as an excuse to rest. When his chest was heaving a little less, he said: 'A small gold statue, Madonna and Child. Silver candlesticks, studded with diamonds, and also a bag of cut stones. That's all.'

Blankers and Raymore had a friendly argument about the value of the hoard. The prisoners started digging again, but without much enthusiasm. After a time, Raymore muttered something. He put down his spade and staggered away to refresh himself. Blankers followed him about five minutes later.

As he was going away, he called back: 'How much further to dig now?'

'A good foot or more,' Sandy gasped, mopping his brow.

'Then keep workin',' the bearded man ordered.

Billy rasped his thumb along his chin, which was prickly. Sandy did the same, but he kept his conversation until Blankers was out of earshot.

He said: 'I suppose you realise Blankers intends this hole for our burial spot, in the event that he finds what he's lookin' for?'

Billy blew salt perspiration off his brow. 'It had occurred to me. An' what's more, if they don't find what they're lookin' for, they won't let us live. At least, Blankers won't an' he's certainly in complete control.'

There was a pause while Sandy

cautiously ascertained how far away from them the four outlaws were. None were very close. All were watchful, but not in any hurry to get to their feet and resume their labours.

'Given the opportunity, would you be prepared to shoot to kill?'

'Of course,' Billy answered brusquely. 'It's the only thing to do when you're dealin' with men crazy-mad with greed!'

'Then your chance is comin' up, amigo. Shift your foot over a little.'

Sandy hurriedly probed in a different spot with his spade, and turned up a piece of cloth. Still going through the motions of ordinary digging, he unrolled the cloth and revealed four revolvers, all well oiled and seemingly ready for instant use.

Billy's eyes almost popped. His thoughts raced back over all the time during which Sandy had kept this a secret. He marvelled at it, and murmured that he was ready, any time.

'There's no treasure here at all, other than these guns, so be ready, amigo. We have the element of surprise, but they outnumber us, an' they're used to tight situations. Wait till they get real close. If anything happens to me head back for the town. The Doc or one of the preachers will fill you in on the rest of the details.'

'I wish you luck, Sandy. You deserve it,' Billy replied warmly. 'An' don't worry about me. I don't need Red Murdo's fate to spur me on. I'm still in this because I want to be.'

A minute or so later, Sandy's spade hit an old tin lid. He thumped it good and hard with the tool a time or two more, and then straightened up, holding his aching back. Billy did the same and took a short breather.

'I think I've struck something, Blankers! This ought to be it!'

Billy watched them come, and marvelled once more at the amount of energy greed could give tired men. He knelt to make the incident look more realistic. Sandy was content to go down on one knee.

16

The two cousins, Drex and Thorn, came along first. In the brief time that this pair had been known to Billy and the Kid, Thorn had never moved so quickly. Lofty was coming from slightly further away, but he had longer legs and he was running as if in a race for a huge prize.

Blankers, the most deadly man of the quartette, was well to the rear and seemingly not bothered about being last. He was on his way, but prepared to let the others have the first look.

When they were less than ten yards away, the prisoners straightened up, side by side and showed the revolvers which had been buried.

Billy's lawman's training made him call out a warning of sorts, even though they were dealing with killers in their most determined mood.

'Hold it right there, all of you! I'm a peace officer, an' these guns are loaded!'

The shock stopped the first three outlaws in their tracks, but not for more than two or three seconds. Suddenly they split and threw themselves sideways, widening the target. While this was happening, the first bullet of the fierce encounter whined across the oasis.

It came from Blankers, the man furthest from the digging area. His guns had appeared in his fists as though they were naturally there. The small missile flew between the parting bodies of Drex and Thorn, and narrowly missed Billy's head. It provided all the prompting that the two young partners needed.

Crouching a little in the pit of sand, they found their own targets and opened up. Billy missed Drex with his first, but drilled him high in the chest with his second. Thorn's first shot singed the Kid's bandanna. Without flinching, Sandy raised himself and blasted off both guns at the homely outlaw. Both shots were effective. He was hit in the left shoulder and in the head at the same time. His body appeared to be lifted a few inches. It settled back, losing the hat, and with the legs bunched up in an awkward position.

Lofty Raymore was more formidable. He fired first at one and then at the other. Without consulting each other, the partners suddenly leapt from the pit and rolled further away, aiming for the trees which gave it cover.

Surprisingly, Blankers had moved further away. As Billy hurled himself behind the tree bole, three bullets from the bearded outlaw's guns came near to ventilating him. One missed behind; the second passed between his knees and the third chipped the tree bole as he made cover.

Billy dropped on his knees and looked for a target. Meanwhile, Sandy, who was prone in the sand, clear of tree cover, pumped shells at Raymore, whose long frame was scarcely concealed by a narrow tree trunk. Raymore replied without scoring a hit, but he panicked and suddenly leapt sideways for better cover.

Billy, looking for Blankers, saw Raymore and hit him twice with his right-hand gun. Lofty made the tree, but he was dying as he sank down out of sight. In the background, horses and mules were prancing about in two tight groups, while Blankers, now on the other side of the water, fired first at one man and then at the other.

The partners continued to go forward. They had been pent up too long to lose the initiative now, especially as they had almost vanquished all the opposition. Probing shots from both men sent the fleeing renegade behind the mules. There, he was afforded some kind of a shield, although neither marksman withheld his fire altogether. Billy worked his way to the left of the pool and Sandy went round to the right.

Between them they ought to pin him down in a short space of time. Blankers, however, frustrated them by acting in a manner which appeared to be entirely contrary to all his nature. All this time, the saddle horses had been walking around with their saddles slackened, but in place.

The bearded man emptied a gun in the direction of Sandy, and at once followed up this act by leaping into the saddle of his roan. While his enemies came to their feet and wondered what would happen next, he spurred the animal towards the edge of the oasis, and deliberately sent it into the desert, heading east.

The partners came breathlessly to the edge of the trees, and fired several parting shots towards him. The roan, however, kept going and soon took him beyond revolver range. He shook his fist at them, and kept on moving.

'Well, Billy, do we go after him?'

'No, we make sure he keeps goin' an' then we retire and tidy up a bit!'

This was the first time that the riding partners realised that most of the tension they had been living with had eased. They clapped one another on the shoulders and hurried to the pool to cool off. After a time, they lifted their faces from the water and prowled the oasis with their guns to hand. All three outlaws had breathed their last, and had died looking uglier than they had in life.

They were pushed into the loot hole with all their hand luggage and solemnly filled in. Their names were scratched out on stones, which were put above them. The victors were flush with four-legged transport and the kind of food which was easily carried.

A fire was lighted. They prepared and ate as good a meal as they could manage, and then thought about the future.

'Do you think Blankers will come back?' Sandy asked.

'I should say so. After all, he doesn't know the loot ain't here,' Billy reasoned. 'I suggest we wait here one night, an' keep a watch for him. After that, we act as if he ain't around any more, and backtrack to Borderville to finish our business with Long John.'

Sandy chuckled. 'I reckon that's downright good figurin', pardner. So until dark, let's rest.'

When they were stretched out in the maximum tree shade, Billy asked: 'Tell me again how you an' Red came by that loot everybody is so interested in.'

'All right,' the Kid agreed. 'Red an' I had rubbed up Carrick's outfit of older renegades, an' they were chasin' us between towns in southern Arizona. When they were not far behind, we happened on an old buildin' which they'd used for years as a hideout. It wasn't a good place to make for, but we needed rest. So we went in, an' we had a bit of luck. Red found a cellar which none of the other men knew about. We got down into it jest before they arrived. They hunted round, an' didn't spot us. They even missed our horses.

'After a time, they went away, an'

before we came up from the cellar, we stumbled on this old loot stached away down there. All we could think of was that it had been put there a long time before by other outlaws. Judgin' by the kind of stuff it was, it had been stolen originally from an old Spanish church.'

Sandy had said all he wanted to say. Billy squinted across at him and nodded several times. 'An' it ain't on this oasis, huh?'

'That's right,' Sandy confirmed.

Billy did not press for further details. He draped his hat over his face and composed himself for sleep.

★   ★   ★

In the last hour of daylight, the friends had another short consultation. It was Billy who asserted himself concerning the possible return of Blankers to the oasis.

'We'll keep a watch, and *I*'ll take the first turn,' he insisted, 'an' you can turn in as soon as you like. If you want my opinion, the best place would be between the horses and the mules on the other side of the pool. I'll stay this side, an' isolate myself a little. If Blankers wants to counter-attack, he'll do it by stealth.'

Sandy stood up and prepared to take the advice. He paused with his bedroll over his shoulder before going off to the new spot.

'I'm glad Della wasn't at the oasis when we had that shoot-up this morning, Billy. She's tough, but she wouldn't have relished that bit of action.'

'My sentiments, too, amigo. She would have been in a funny position, too, having ridden here with the opposition.'

Sandy nodded and sighed. 'Life sure has been complicated of late, but it could have been much worse.'

He wandered off, kicking at a stone.

*   *   *

Blankers started back towards the tantalising oasis just before sundown.

An hour after dusk, he was several hundred yards away sitting his horse and wondering how best he could regain control of the water hole and the two determined young men who had won it.

He was a tough, hardened and resourceful criminal, but since he took up the trail of the Coyote Kids, he had met with setbacks. First, there was that abortive attempt to get information out of Red Murdo, which had resulted in Murdo's death — without learning anything worthwhile.

Now, he had reached the actual burial spot of the treasure, only to be bested by two young men who had been prisoners, and who would have been dead and buried by now, but for a clever trick pulled by one of them. Sandy East and Billy Bartram had been costly to the Carrick outfit. They had caused him — Blankers — to lose face with his Boss. Only a complete reversal of the present position, and a return with the treasure intact would suffice to put the top gun back in favour.

He hoped that the fates would not let him down on this vital occasion. Two hundred yards nearer the gently waving cluster of trees he dismounted, poured the last dregs of brackish water from his canteen into his hat and gave them to the parched roan. The horse drank greedily, but apparently expected to be allowed to visit the water hole without delay.

Blankers talked persuasively to it, and left it secured to a large rock, with the saddle slackened again. Armed with his twin .44s and a Remington, he moved forward with great caution, prepared to do the best stalking job of his career. After all, the possible rewards had never been so high.

One hundred yards away, he started to crawl. His task was a difficult one. He had to approach so quietly that two men, and several horses and mules would not be disturbed. He began to theorise about the best way to do it. He tried to read the minds of the pair who were probably on the lookout for him.

They would probably leave the horses and mules in one half of the oasis and spread themselves out on the other. Yard by yard, he cut down on the desired spot. As he came close, he could see that the mules and horses were in two separate groups. He began to get the idea that he might be able to creep between the two groups of animals, and thus enter the water hole from a direction no one would anticipate.

He warmed to the idea, difficult though it would be to put into practice. His throat, by now, was quite dry, and his tongue was almost stuck to the roof of his mouth. But his resolution was unwavering. Up through the two groups, slake the thirst and then a careful attack on the two young men. After that, plain sailing . . .

None of the animals stirred sufficiently to give him away. He was five yards from the water's edge when a sort of sixth sense warned him that one of his enemies was closer than he had anticipated. He became perfectly still, and glanced around him. About twenty feet away to his right, he saw the still form of a sleeper, and he knew that his reading of the other men's minds had failed.

Here was one of them, stretched out and sleeping peacefully between the animal groups. Blankers clamped down on his gripping thirst. He still had the advantage of surprise, and he would use it to the best of his ability. He laid down his Remington, which had been tiring his arm, and also discarded one of his .44s. This had to be a silent job, if the second enemy was not to be alerted before he was ready for him.

Pulling his belt knife, he started towards the sleeper, moving slowly and squirming like a huge tailless lizard. Some five feet away, the slim figure, half buried in a sheepskin vest and a soiled Texas-style hat, stirred in sleep.

'Billy?' came the whisper. 'Billy, what in tarnation are you playin' at?'

The voice had become almost imperceptibly louder. Blankers attempted to impersonate the young deputy. 'Get back to sleep, Sandy, it ain't time yet!'

His voice was no louder, but he did his best to ensure that it carried better. Sandy made some sort of a noise which suggested that he was satisfied with the reply. Just as he appeared to be settling down again, however, he shrugged his shoulders, lifted his hat off his face and shot one quick glance at the person he knew was near him.

Blankers knew that he had been recognised. He sprang and closed with the young man who had so frustrated him. East arched his back and rolled away from the sharp blade which was almost at his throat.

* * *

A slight noise carried to Billy Bartram on the other side of the water. He blinked himself awake, having dozed, and leapt as though he had been stung.

Something was wrong across the pool. There was a scuffle. Horses were snickering. One had risen to its feet. A mule was braying and two of the cross-bred animals were threatening to start a fight.

Billy called: 'Sandy! What's wrong?'

There was no reply, other than the sound of a body, or bodies, rolling about in the soft sand. In a flash, the young deputy realised that their enemy had crept in unnoticed. He had fallen down in his watch-keeping and given his partner into the hands of his enemy.

Rising to his feet, Billy scrubbed his tousled fair hair and massaged his face. Gripping a .45 in each fist he went straight down the slight slope, into the water, and waded through it towards the other side. As he drew nearer he could hear the harsh breathing of the two men struggling in the sand. Backwards and forwards they rolled, one trying to use his weapon and the other fighting for his life.

Billy guessed how things were.

Blankers had slipped in unnoticed, and he would have the upper hand. The wrestling went on, with both men so close together that any sort of shooting might kill the wrong man. Perspiring with worry and a feeling of guilt, Billy waited his chance with growing impatience.

Sandy gasped, the action slowed, and a few seconds later, they were rolling in the other direction, towards the ill-tempered mules. Over and over the wrestlers rolled, until they had some-how passed under the belly of one beast and arrived directly behind two others which were quarrelling.

Blankers was breathing very hard by now. He sought to free his knife arm long enough to use it effectively just once. Sandy, meanwhile, clung on. In seeking to release his arms, the outlaw rose to his feet. At the same time, Sandy's grip slipped, leaving the knife man free.

Roaring with triumph, Blankers barged one mule. He drew back his arm to deal a death blow. The blade was flashing forward, out of sight of Billy, when the nearest mule suddenly lashed out with both its hind legs. One hoof connected with the side of Blankers head with sudden and sickening force.

The vicious knife attack lost momentum. Sandy was able to roll aside and draw breath, while Blankers slumped where he had been. The outlaw's head nodded the ground three or four times. He thrashed about for upwards of ten seconds, and then subsided, dead.

Billy sprang forward then, clearing the water and dropping beside Blankers. He put a revolver against the man's ear, and raised the head by the hair, the hat being elsewhere. The skull was crushed by the mule kick. A few yards away, the animals fought on, totally unaware of the remarkable change they had wrought in the men's affairs.

Billy lowered the head to the ground and flopped beside his partner, looking him over with genuine concern. Sandy's main trouble was abject tiredness coupled with lack of breath. He had a hair scratch on his neck, a similar one down the left side of his face and a trickle of blood across the back of one hand. His sheepskin vest had a knife cut down it from neck to waist. It remained in one piece, held almost literally by a thread.

'Is — is there any wound I can't see?' Billy queried, tense with anguish.

'No, none at all, amigo, don't upset yourself.' Sandy crawled to the water's edge and flopped when he was just close enough to drink.

17

Two days had elapsed when Billy and the Kid rode back into Borderville from the south. They had with them the horses and mules, but no bodies. The spare horses were left at a rail outside the livery near the south end.

It was clear that many of the townsfolk were not at their accustomed work. A Mexican livery hand was the one to put them in the picture.

'My friends, almost everyone is at the cemetery. They are attending the funeral of the tall man, the one who came with the *gringo* riders. The doctor treated him, an' the woman nursed him, but alas, he died. You will see how it is.'

Feeling rather shaken, the partners left their horses in the livery hand's care and walked out into the bright morning sunlight.

Billy remarked: 'Long John Carrick is dead?'

'He was the only one who stayed behind with the woman,' Sandy reminded him.

Together, they walked through the pleasant town, and presently they encountered the people coming back from the burial ground. Della had had no black gown with her when she started on the ride south, but she was wearing one now. The newcomers stepped into the stream of mourners, and lined up on either side of Della, who nodded gravely to them.

For the moment, she had no thought for the men who had trekked further south after her brother and his friend with greed and murder in their hearts. Gradually, the sober-faced townsfolk dispersed. Della and her escorts walked on to the church with the bell. It was empty at that time, and comparatively cool within.

'Boys, if you'll excuse me for a minute, I think I'll go in there an' try to put my feelings in order.'

She smiled at them rather nervously, and nodded to the two preachers and the doctor who were following up behind. Sandy laid a hand on Billy's arm, detaining him under the shadowy arch, while Della entered alone.

Billy was very curious as to what had happened since they left town. He opened the conversation by revealing the fate, very briefly, of the outlaws who had ridden south to get the loot and eliminate them.

'Long John was taken ill, on arrival?' he questioned.

The doctor nodded. 'Almost right away. He was a sick man, had been for some time. High, reckless living over a long period, followed by prison food and a hard routine, had taken their toll of his constitution. His heart an' circulation had gone back on him. And then the sunstroke aggravated his general debility. He took to a bed in my house, and was tended by Mrs Rhodes, who, I understand, is Sandy's sister.'

Sandy seemed awfully jumpy about

something. He asked: 'And did she nurse him well, Doc? It's important for me to know this.'

'All the time I was around, she acted the part of a first-class nurse, Sandy. Only it wasn't enough. Recent happenings seem to have changed her. None of us know her mind right now. Maybe you ought to go in there an' talk to her, eh? We'll wait around until you come out.'

The Kid sighed, but he nodded and took their advice. As soon as he had gone, Billy stepped closer to the doctor. 'Doc, I'd like to know the whole truth. Did Della do, or fail to do anything at all which had a bearing on Carrick's death? Sandy doesn't have to know, an' I won't pass on anything you tell me now.'

Dr Scott became suddenly thoughtful, rubbing the limb on which he limped. He glanced briefly at Father Ignatius and the Reverend Myett. In answer to his quizzical raising of the eyebrows, each of them nodded.

'All right, I'll tell you. I thought that with careful handlin' Carrick might have pulled through this crisis in his life. His recovery all depended upon some rather vital medicine I made up for him. I'll never be able to prove this, but I believe Mrs Rhodes withheld the dosage when Carrick needed it most.'

'Thank you for tellin' me, Doc. I think I might go in now an' talk with the other two.'

The trio of senior townsmen signified their approval. Billy walked into the church and soon adjusted to the semi-gloom. Sandy and Della were sitting in a pew about three rows in from the door. Hatless, he moved in beside them.

Sandy was saying: 'So you see there hasn't been any loot buried for a long time. It's here, in this town, most of it in this church — the sort of place it was originally stolen from. Up there, around the altar, are the silver candlesticks, and high up in that wall niche is the miniature figure of the Madonna and

Child, wrought in gold.'

Della was looking up and around her, wide-eyed with wonder. Billy was not so surprised, having already guessed where the buried treasure had come to rest.

'And the bag of diamonds,' Sandy resumed, 'is in the hands of the three men who make the decisions for the town. It is being used indirectly to pay ordinary men for their labours, until such time as prosperity is attracted to this out of the way place. If you want any sort of a share in it, however, there is a way. You'd have to settle here, and become a useful member of the community. A lot of things have happened to you lately, but when your head clears, you ought to think seriously about whether you can settle here.

'For my part, I quit Borderville once, but that was when Red was alive. I shan't go north again. My future lies here. I'll do what I can to make the town a prosperous place. I'm thankful to be still alive after the events of the past few weeks.'

Silently, the three rose to their feet and left the building.

* * *

The crude wooden ladder which had lain along the bottom of the south wall of the church had not been tested by the Mexican workmen who had been building it with tree branches, leather thongs and short cross members. The figure of the person who came out at dark and borrowed it was shrouded in a dark cloak. It took a little time to carry the ladder indoors and set it against the wall under the niche, but it was in place at last.

Rung by rung the slim, cloaked figure climbed it towards the beautifully fashioned gold figures. Billy Bartram ghosted into the church unnoticed when the climb was half completed. Three rungs away from the coveted trophy a cross-member slipped. The figure lost balance, let out a terrified female shriek and fell straight to the stone floor below, where life left the body instantly.

Billy ran bootless to the fallen figure, and knelt beside it. He was glad that Sandy had not been present to witness Della's tragic end. Her ungovernable greed had brought about her downfall. The hand which tapped him on the shoulder was that of Father Ignatius, who had also arrived in time to witness the lethal accident.

The priest covered the body with the cloak after saying a brief prayer over it. He intimated that he wanted Billy to help him remove the ladder. They did this between them, and some time later, retired full of regret.

*   *   *

It was suggested the following morning to Sandy that his sister had merely wanted to take a closer look at the beautiful wrought gold figures when the accident occurred. If he doubted the

261

veracity of the explanation, he never openly said so.

The whole town backed him at Della's funeral, and the following day Billy prepared to depart alone. At the point in town furthest west, he finally shook hands with the surviving Coyote Kid.

'I think you're right to stay here, Sandy. I'm goin' to deliver certain information regardin' Carrick and his gang, an' then I'll finish ridin' as a deputy and come back here. I'd like to have a hand in the buildin' of Borderville, an' somehow I think my Pa would approve. Adios, amigo, an' you, too, gentlemen.'

The senior townsmen backing the Kid acted as though they knew he would be back. Billy had a notion, too, that they understood the deep loneliness occasioned by the parting of the ways.

We do hope that you have enjoyed reading this large print book.

Did you know that all of our titles are available for purchase?

We publish a wide range of high quality large print books including:
**Romances, Mysteries, Classics
General Fiction
Non Fiction and Westerns**

Special interest titles available in large print are:
**The Little Oxford Dictionary
Music Book, Song Book
Hymn Book, Service Book**

Also available from us courtesy of Oxford University Press:
**Young Readers' Dictionary
(large print edition)
Young Readers' Thesaurus
(large print edition)**

For further information or a free brochure, please contact us at:
**Ulverscroft Large Print Books Ltd.,
The Green, Bradgate Road, Anstey,
Leicester, LE7 7FU, England.
Tel:** (00 44) **0116 236 4325**
Fax: (00 44) **0116 234 0205**

Other titles in the
Linford Western Library:

RIDE BACK TO REDEMPTION

Eugene Clifton

After a bank raid robbed him of his wife and unborn child, Jeff Warrinder, sheriff of Redemption, ended up a drunken no-hoper. Working off a debt to Cassie Hanson, he gets tangled up in her feud with Bull Krantz. Meanwhile, the new sheriff is in deep trouble, whilst Krantz's gang of outlaws is after Jeff's blood. If he's ever to make the ride back to Redemption, Jeff must overcome his own demon: the one that comes in a whisky bottle.

MARSHAL LAW

Corba Sunman

Deputy Marshal Jed Law was sent to Buffalo Crossing to keep the peace; a bloody feud between two ranchers had already cost a man his life. But Law's real troubles started when he first set eyes on Julie Rutherford and her father Ben . . . Opposed by hard cases determined to wipe him out, he would be forced to shoot his way through. And worse was to come . . . Law would need his pistol loaded and ready to use until the last desperate shot.

HOT LEAD RANGE

Jack Holt

When an undercover agent going by the name of Bob Harker arrives in Sweetwater Valley, his task is to prevent a range war developing: the ruthless Butch Collins intends to claim the entire valley by forcing out his neighbours. One such neighbour is Frank Bateman — Harker's old boss when he was a Pinkerton detective. Harker manages to infiltrate the Collins outfit but, forced to take ever greater risks, could this be his final mission?